NEW BEGINNINGS

BETTY BRADFORD

New Beginnings
Copyright © 2023 by Betty Bradford

All rights reserved. No part of this publication may be reproduced, distributed, or transmitted in any form or by any means, including photocopying, recording, or other electronic or mechanical methods, without the prior written permission of the author, except in the case of brief quotations embodied in critical reviews and certain other non-commercial uses permitted by copyright law.

Tellwell Talent
www.tellwell.ca

ISBN
978-1-77941-076-4 (Paperback)

New Beginnings

"Bedtime sweetheart." said Sam as he shooed his daughter to her room.

"Aww dad, exclaimed Becky, can you and mom tuck me in?"

"You know, we always do." replied Sam.

"I know, can you and mom read me a bedtime story?"

"So, who will get to read you the story tonight?" asked Sarah, Becky's mom.

"You can, mom, but dad can help; I like the story about Grampie Carl, when he hit his head on the car ceiling!"

Becky was five years old, and she was an only child. Her dad, Sam was a Certified Carpenter and Writer. Sarah, her mom worked as a caregiver at a local nursing home.

"Sam, where is your book?" questioned Sarah.

"In my office, near the typewriter, why?" questioned Sam.

"I want to read it, ok." added Sarah.

Chapter One

The Larsen family were anticipating an exciting move from Denmark to Canada! Carlos was always searching for greener pastures. The family had experienced an earlier move to France; However, Carlos became disillusioned with the French style of farming. Back to Denmark they went; Back to Denmark to live with Carlos' rich mom. She lived on a villa in Copenhagen. Carlos loved it there, and would love to stay, despite the fact, Stella hated it. No matter how big the house, there is never enough room for two women. Carlos could not stand the bickering so, he wrote a letter to his sister, Elizabeth for some ideas. Elizabeth was a single woman, living in California; And she was rich!

Elizabeth knew about Canada and, she suggested to Carlos, that he should move to British Columbia. There, he could take up farming like so many people did there. The farmlands were rich and productive.

Well, Carlos started to make plans to travel to Canada. He arranged for his family to meet him there after a couple of months.

Carlos was anticipating the excitement of new beginnings, as he boarded The United States Scandinavian Lines to Canada. His mind was racing, with many ideas.

Onboard the ship, Carlos exchanged a conversation with Arthur Svenson. Arthur was from New Denmark, Canada; He was returning from a visit in Denmark. "You're going to British Columbia." he said to Carlos, dragging a long breath through his pipe.

"Ya, Carlos replied, my sister said it would be a good place to do some farming."

"Ya, that would be but, let me tell you about New Denmark." said Arthur.

"New Denmark was founded by some Danish immigrants to North America." explained Arthur; It's kinda like living in Denmark. Most of us speak Danish, and many of us retain our Danish culture. "What do you think, Carlos?"

"I think I'm changing my destination; New Denmark, here I come!"

Carlos arrived at Pier 21, Halifax, after ten days aboard a crowded ship. He was exhausted!

Now he will seek new beginnings in New Denmark, land of rolling hills and farmland to no end.

Arthur did not tell Carlos, however, that he had to invest a good portion of his savings to purchase a hundred and eighty acres of land. There was a run-down farmhouse and a couple of barns on the property. Carlos had his work cut out for him for the next two months, before he planned for his family's arrival.

When Stella and the boys docked at Pier 21 Halifax, Peter and Carl were detained for fifteen days. They contracted the German measles aboard ship, and Stella and Neils had to leave them behind, and board a train to Moncton.

"Peter, said Carl, I'm scared, are you?"

"Nah, replied Peter, just follow me." A security officer took their bags and led them to a small room, and he filled out some forms. And then, some guy, dressed in a white coat and mask, brought them to a room with a couple of cots, a table and two chairs. This was where they had to stay for the time being.

Carl was hungry, and before he got a chance to say so, the man in the white coat and mask brought them a tray full of food, and some utensils. "Oh boy, this is good!" said Carl.

"Yeah, it is, agreed Peter, I was hungry."

After the fifteen days, the security officer brought them to a model T car, their ride to the train station. The ride was bumpy; sometimes they almost hit the ceiling.

The driver looked at them in his rear-view mirror and laughed to himself.

About eight hours later, their dad, Carlos met them in a village called Plaster Rock; He came with horse and buggy. Were they ever happy to see their dad. They talked non-stop all the way to New Denmark. "Dad, said Carl, I almost hit my head in that car," and Peter finished describing their ride.

When Carlos and the boys got home, Stella had a steaming hot meal waiting for them. Neils, their brother should have been in bed, but under the circumstances, he got to stay up.

CHAPTER TWO

It was early fall; Harvest time was one of the major times of the year. There was vegetables and fruit to harvest for sale and home use. There was wood to be cut, and sold for stove wood, and for Carlos's mill.

Stella found this new land very difficult. She found little time to indulge in the finer things of Denmark. She was now, fully occupied with meals, household chores, and helping Carlos to manage the farm. Handiwork, such as knitting and crochet, became a necessity. There would be socks, mittens, and underwear to knit. There were cows to milk, and butter to churn. The work was endless!

Carlos, too, enjoyed his woodworking skill in Denmark. Now, his hobby became a necessity. There was furniture to be made and sold, to earn money to purchase farm machinery. The mill took up many hours of his time, also. The work running the farm was more than Carlos had anticipated.

Depression days were soon upon them. The economy was declining rapidly, regardless, how hard they worked.

Living on a farm, meant families were self- sufficient, however, some things, like coffee and tea, were purchased with food stamps.

There was talk of World War Two. Everyone listened intently to their radios during the evenings.

Carlos began to experience some health issues; Pain like he never experienced before. "What's the matter, Carlos?" asked Stella.

"I don't know." he replied to Stella bending over and holding on to his abdomen.

"We gotta get Doc Brown; He may have some answers." Stella said.

"Maybe it will go away, I'll see Doc later." said Carlos. Well, the pain did not go away; It got worse. Doc Brown came and gave Carlos some pain medication. He called Stella outside on the porch and, told her that Carlos would not be getting better. It would be, just a matter of time.

Carlos made it to spring the next year. The past few months after his diagnosis were very difficult, lot of pain, suffering and heartache.

Now, with no savings left and a bill for funeral expenses, Stella was devastated more than ever in her life! She found a job doing housework for a rich couple living in Grand Falls, a nearby town.

New Beginnings

Peter was married, and he and his wife had a family. Neils was working at his dad's mill during the day, and on the farm during the evenings. Carl assumed the rest of the responsibility of the farm.

Chapter Three

WWII had begun. It was 1939, and Carl enlisted with The Carleton York Regiment, and they were sent to Europe.

One can never prepare for war; However, Carl had the ability to endure a crisis, and adapt to major changes in his life. He was an amazing young man, and an amazing soldier. He was a front-line soldier, which meant his life, and the lives of fellow troops depended on his intuitive ideas and choices. Once, the troops arrived in France, the Germans had their strategic plans put into action.

Everyone from the Carleton York was shot, and presumed dead. Everyone, except Carl; He vividly recalls the incident. He was near a stoop of grain at the back of a barn when the Germans opened fire. Carl dropped to the ground; He was shot in the leg.

Carl was taken as a prisoner of war; There would no longer be letters, or money sent to Stella. Everyone would take for granted that Carl died in action. Carl's mom and his brothers held a memorial for him, and everyone carried on as usual, until the war ended in 1945.

Everyone listened intently to their radios, regarding everything post war. Many soldiers would not be returning, and many that did, suffered physical and psychological disabilities. The war left a lasting mark on everyone. The Government compensated for these pangs of war through The Royal Canadian Legion, and The Department of Veterans Affairs. There was respite from The Canadian Red Cross, veteran hospitals, pension, and other funds providing soldiers with a means for a new beginning!

A telegraph arrived at Stella's door; These words she read, with blurring eyes, "Carl sent to veteran hospital, Saint John, NB." Stella became weak at her knees and started to tremble. She could not wait to share the good news with Neils and Peter! Carl was alive, and he would be home soon!

As exciting as it was, Carl got home, a changed man. He experienced nightmares, angry outbursts, and then, there would be the quiet times when, he just starred! It would be months before the real Carl would emerge again!

Chapter Four

A new year brought new beginnings. New beginnings for Carl with a young lady, named Katherine. She was a teenager when war started, and now, she had blossomed into a beautiful young lady. Her hair was black and, her eyes were blue like blueberries; Her lips were the color of strawberries. That is how Carl described her.

Katherine lived on a huge farm owned by Yvon and Evangeline Derosier. She had sixteen siblings, so, they were a very busy family.

After evening chores, everyone, except Mrs. Derosier, would sit around the table to play cards. Mrs. Derosier, Eva, sat in her rocking chair, listening to a French radio station, while she clicked her knitting needles together.

Sometimes Carl and Katherine went to the dances in New Denmark, and sometimes, they took long walks and shared their hopes and dreams. They were in love!

New Beginnings

The young couple planned on getting married soon, however, they were met with family opposition. Carl was Protestant and Katherine was Catholic. At the time, these religious differences would not stop the couple from pursuing their plans to marry. They decided to elope!

Carl bought his first new car, a 1947 Chevy! Oh, how his friends, and of course, Katherine loved that car! Now, they could drive around in style and, become the talk of the community! Yes, and soon there would be more.

"Katherine, said Carl, I'm going to Toronto this weekend."

"And, added Katherine, what about me?"

"I'll send you a letter after I find a job." he said.

Katherine started to sob angry tears, "What about our plans?"

"We will still get married, and after I make enough money, I will come and get you. Then, we will go back to Toronto and get married."

Katherine was still not happy, but she lightened up after Carl teased and kissed her.

The next day, Carl left for Toronto and, eighteen hours later, he was city-center. He checked into a hotel for the night. He bought a local newspaper, found a list of apartments, and job listings. There was a big demand for carpenters; He would find an apartment or boarding place, the next day. Then, he would apply for a job. Not surprisingly, he moved into a boarding house that next afternoon. Then, he had to be on site for his new job interview the next morning.

Chapter Five

Carl got employed at City Builders' Inc.; His new boss was Jack Grey, an ex-army officer. "Good morning Carl, follow me; I'll show you around." he said.

Carl proved his work ethics on his first day, and Jack knew he would become an honest, reliable and hard-working employee. He became a great co-worker, and he was making friends. At night, he wrote letters to Katherine, to keep her up to date, regarding his plans to continue their relationship. He was happy; Katherine kept responding to Carl's letters, but she did not tell him, she had a new boyfriend. She met Eugene at a dance in New Denmark, a month after Carl left, and she did not know how to tell him.

Six months later, and with twelve hundred dollars in his pocket, Carl was on his way to New Denmark. He was excited and, he wanted to surprise Katherine. The first place he visited was his mom's. Stella met him at the door; She heard him drive up. She gave him a quick hug and, offered him a coffee.

"Thanks mom, but I am in a hurry. He set his duffel bag down by the entryway, tipped his cap, and headed out the door. He could not wait to see Katherine.

He knocked on Mr. Derosiers' door, good and loud. Eva came to the door with a wooden spoon in her hand; She was busy mixing up some molasses cookies.

"Mrs. Derosier, is Katherine home?" he asked.

Eva got nervous and, started to stutter, "She's at Stanley Neilson's; She's keeping house there."

"Thanks, Mrs. Derosier." he said, as he closed her door. He was in the Neilson driveway a few minutes later. He hurried to their front door and knocked. Katherine came to the door, and when she saw Carl, her face turned pale. She knew, she had to tell Carl about Eugene; There was not time to avoid doing so. Carl became livid, slammed the door and practically ran to his car. He got in, spun his wheels on the gravel, and headed to Peters'. Peter would listen to him, and he would be very supportive.

Carl knocked on Peters' door, and Aaron opened the door, and yelled, "It's Uncle Carl!" Peter came out right away, and welcomed him in. "Martha, get us a coffee, and join us in the living room, we got some catching up to do." Peter knew Katherine was dating Eugene, so he got right to the point. "Sorry about Katherine; She started dating Eugene not long after you left."

Aaron kept trying to gain Carl's attention, and he talked incessantly. "Aaron, said Peter, go play; You can visit with Uncle Carl later." Aaron lowered his head and muttered to himself as he left the room.

"I'm hurting bad right now Peter, and I won't stay too long; I want to spend a few minutes with Aaron, before I leave." Then, he went outside, found a ball on the ground, and got Aaron to play catch. "Hey, you are getting good at this!' he remarked.

"Well, we play catch at school." said Aaron.

"Oh yeah, what grade are you in now?" asked Carl.

"Grade five," he answered and, threw the ball back.

"Wow, Aaron, I'm proud of you, give me five, and I gotta go".

"Awww Uncle Carl, so soon?" he asked as he gave his uncle his high five.

Carl left to return to his mom's place. He wanted to spend the weekend with her before he returned to Toronto. She might need him to help her around the house.

Sunday afternoon came quickly, and Carl was leaving for Toronto. "You take care, Carl, said his mother as he was leaving. Have a safe trip back and, call me when you get home, ok?" Stella had tears in her eyes; She turned around and, picked up a tin of cookies from the counter and, passed them to him. She hated to see him leave, especially this time.

Chapter Six

There are always new beginnings to anticipate. Carl was feeling depressed and lonely, after he got back to his Toronto home. It was too quiet and empty, so he took his things inside, turned around and left. There would be some guys down at the bowling alley, perhaps. Maybe a few bottles of beer with the guys would cheer him up.

Just when he walked into the bowling alley, his Coworker and now buddy, called him over to a table. "Didn't expect to see you so soon." he said.

"Well, here I am, ready or not." he added. He did not want to talk about Katherine.

The guys sipped on their beer, did some small talk, and they kidded each other between rounds in their game. Soon it was time to return home; Everybody had to be at work the next day, except Carl. He still had a few days of vacation left. The new house that he purchased a week ago needed some minor repairs and a few personal touches;

He kept himself busy with the house, and before long, he was back at work.

"Welcome back, Carl." Said Jack as he put his hand on his shoulder. He already knew about Katherine jilting him. "We got a new contract coming up Carl, he said. I think you will like working on this one, an old mansion of a house."

"When do I get to see it?" he asked.

"Just when we finish this one, in a few days." replied Jack.

The mansion of a house was well-dilapidated. But, with time and a lot of work, they could have the job done by Christmas.

New Market Realty bought the house for resale; Nicole Lemieux owned the real estate company. Nicole was a strong-willed and determined woman. She expected perfection from everyone she dealt with and, there were no excuses for otherwise.

Nicole was very young and attractive. She had long black hair pulled back tightly in a pug, and she exuded a strong air of confidence and professionalism.

Jack called his employees to his attention on the first morning of their new contract. "Guys, I hope you will all enjoy working this new project. I have only one concern to address. This Nicole is to be ignored; I do not want any whistles or whatever coming from you, comprehendo!"

Jack had assessed the house for repairs. Carl, you can take the main floor and Johnathan, you can start on the roof. Fred, you and Mitchell can go to the second floor.

The men went straight to work; They had six hours left to work for that day.

Jack met the guys again, before work the next day. "Good morning, guys, just wanted to let you know that I am parking my trailer here until the end of this contract. If you have any concerns or needs, you can come to see me at the trailer. I will be on location occasionally."

After a week into the project, Nicole decided to visit. She, with Jack by her side, was approaching the building. She held a clipboard in her hand, looking very professional. Carl kept watching them from his peripheral field of vision; He was avoiding any eye contact, while he worked away.

Then, one day, the inevitable happened. Nicole was not aware of all the potential danger inside the old mansion. "Ahhh," she sounded; Then, she moaned in extreme pain. Carl heard her sounds, but he did not think that she had been injured. He continued working and then, he heard, "Help!" He searched upstairs for Nicole; She was sitting on the floor with one leg below the floor. She was experiencing critical pain.

"Nicole, can I help?" Carl got down on his knees to assess her injury and then, he retreated to the trailer to get Jack. Unfortunately, Jack was not around; When he returned to Nicole, Fred was by her side. Together, they got her up, took her to Jack's trailer and, called an ambulance.

Nicole's leg was broken, and the doctor applied a plaster cast. She would not be visiting the work site any time soon.

"Hello Jack, do you have Carl's phone number; I want to personally say thank-you to him." said Nicole.

Nicole needed some help, and Carl had been kind enough to offer his services. "Thank you, Carl, for your offer to help; I need another favor, I need to go for a check-up at the hospital, can you take me?"

"Yeah, when?" he replied.

Soon, Nicole and Carl saw each other often, and soon, they were dating.

Chapter Seven

Nicole and Carl had been dating for three months; They took in the cinema once a week, went to fine restaurants and some small diners as well. They went for short walks and stargazed whenever they had a chance. Other than occupying their time at work, they spent their time with each other.

"Nicole, what are your plans for the weekend?" asked Carl.

"Nothing special, she replied, why?"

"Well, I thought you might like a weekend in the country."

"Yeah, I'll start packing now!" she replied.

"Just be sure you pack some bug repellant; We might go fishing!" replied Carl.

The couple had a terrific time, despite fly bites and sunburn. "Do you want to do this again, Nicole? asked Carl, I'm having a blast!"

"Yeah, just don't push me in the brook, again!" she replied with a small giggle.

"I really didn't push you; I saw that you were sliding on the wet grass, so I tried to keep you from falling in." said Carl. Then, they were both laughing.

December first, at six am., on a Monday morning, everyone woke up to five inches of snow on the ground, roof tops, and trees; A beauty to behold, created by Mother Nature, herself. Nicole called Carl. "Did you look outside?" she asked. Carl sounded grumpy; He had just gotten up.

"Yeah, he replied, I'll have to go out, clean off the car, and shovel off the walk".

"Oh, poor Carl, teased Nicole, do you want me to come over, and help you?"

Carl replied, "Goodbye Nicole." And he hung up.

The arrival of winter meant Christmas was just around the bend. Nicole's dad, Samuel Lemieux was in France, so Nicole would have had to spend the holidays alone. Luckily, she would have Carl spending the holidays this year with her.

Sam was sixty-eight years old and lived with Nicole since his wife died a couple of years ago. Sam was struggling with loneliness and depression, still; He decided to visit in France this winter. His father, Joseph Lemieux came from the old country, and Sam always had a desire to visit places his dad spoke off.

Before Sam moved to Toronto, he and his family lived in a small community of Bluebell, NB. He worked on the CNR railroad, and he got transferred to Toronto. Nicole was ten years old, then. And not long after their move to Toronto, her mother died. Now, at twenty, she and Carl were sharing their stories about New Brunswick.

"Well Nicole, why don't we go to New Denmark and spend Christmas, there? Mom would be thrilled; We could even go tree hunting in the woods." Suggested Carl.

"And go skiing, and sliding, and skating," she added. They packed and loaded up the car and, seventeen hours later, they were at Stellas' place.

Carl was excited about introducing Nicole to his mom and family; He was so proud of her. "Mom, this is my gorgeous girlfriend, Nicole".

"Nice to meet you, Mrs. Larsen." Nicole said, reaching out her hand, for a handshake.

Stella turned down the handshake, and gave her a quick hug, instead. Later, Stella and Nicole were baking Danish pastries, cookies and breads. They also baked some of Nicole's favorites like, Tourtiere, French meat pie. For Christmas supper, they served turkey with stuffing, mashed potatoes with gravy, and various vegetables. One of the Danish favorites was red cabbage, which did not appeal to Nicole. After the main course, they enjoyed Danish Apple Cake for dessert. Now, that went over well with everyone. "I'm so full, I think I could burst!" commented Carl. "How about going for a walk, Nicole?"

"Yeah, I'd love to, said Nicole, but first, I'm helping your mom with the dishes."

"You go for a walk with Carl, said Stella, I can do the dishes."

"No mom, said Carl, Nicole's right, we will help with the dishes first."

The night was cold, and the air was fresh. Nicole and Carl walked in step with each other, holding hands. Together, they started to ask, "Did you see that?"

"A falling star." Carl said.

"The sky is just beautiful, I'm so glad you asked me for a walk." said Nicole. They gave each other a quick hug and kiss before they headed back to the house. After getting back, they sat with Stella and some family members, reminiscing and telling stories. They were having a wonderful time.

The time went by quickly and, soon they had to return to Toronto. It was too soon for Stella; However, this visit gave her a renewed sense of family love and togetherness. Carl and Nicole left early in the morning, after Stella served breakfast.

"It's better to get away with a full stomach, she said. Again, she had tears overflowing her eyes, as she hugged Carl and Nicole. Goodbye," she said, and she waved to them in their car until they were out of sight.

Chapter Eight

It was early morning when Carl and Nicole arrived home in Toronto. For that reason, Carl stayed with Nicole at her place. They were going to give Sam a call to wish him a Happy New Year. "Dad, how are you?" asked Nicole.

"Great Nicole, how are you and Carl?"

"We're fine, we just got back from New Denmark." said Nicole.

"Did you enjoy your visit, despite the cold?" asked Sam.

"Yeah dad, we ate until we were stuffed; The food was so...... good, and dad, we went for a walk."

Sam was having a hard time getting a chance to say something. "And dad, the stars in New Denmark filled the sky at night. You should have seen them!"

"Could I speak to Carl, please?" asked Sam. Nicole passed the phone over to Carl.

"Hi Sam, how are you doing?"

"Fine, how is Nicole managing at the house, asked Sam; You know, I worry about her."

"Fine", responded Carl, as he passed the phone back to Nicole.

"Happy New Year, dad!" She exclaimed.

"Happy New Year to you and Carl, love you!" said Sam.

"Love you too, dad." said Nicole as she hung up the phone. For a few minutes later, Nicole was quiet, so Carl remained quiet also. A lot of thoughts and different emotions was flooding their minds right then.

Nicole spoke first, "Did dad say something about me?"

"Well, said Carl; Well, he wanted to know how you were managing, regarding the house."

"I wonder why he didn't ask me." She added. Carl did not say anything more; He did not think he needed to tell her that, her father was worrying about her.

Everyone got into a normal routine again, until the Easter weekend, approaching. Carl was hoping to go to New Denmark again, and he had hopes that Nicole would join him. "Nicole, could we make plans to go to New Denmark for a long weekend?" he asked.

"I want to take in the Good Friday, and the Easter services at my church; I've been keeping Lent over the past forty days." said Nicole. Carl felt guilty; He hadn't given God any thought at all for a very long time. "And remember, dad should be coming home soon." added Nicole.

"When is he coming home?" asked Carl.

"Well, said Nicole, he did not say, but dad is like that. He likes to surprise me."

Sam was flying in on a Thursday night. He was keeping a big surprise from Nicole; He had gotten married and, he did not know how Nicole would react to the news. Marguerite and Sam had been secretly dating, and the real reason for their trip to France was their honeymoon.

After Marguerite's husband passed away a year ago, she and Sam started dating. They did not feel comfortable sharing the news of their relationship, just yet. Sam called from the Toronto airport, to prepare Nicole for his arrival. He hired a taxi to take Marguerite to her home first; He was not prepared to tell Nicole of their marriage, yet.

Nicole heard the taxi on the gravel. She ran out the door to greet her dad and to give him a big bear hug.

'Ok, ok Nicole." said Sam as he worked himself free, because she was hugging him too tight.

Nicole grabbed one of her fathers' suitcases and together, they walked up the drive and into the house. Sam looked around the living room; He missed his home. "Dad, while you catch your breath, and freshen up, I'll call Carl and tell him you are home."

"Yeah sure, I'm looking forward to meet him." Sam headed upstairs to his room, and Nicole made her phone call.

"Hey Carl, dad's home and he wants to meet you. Can you come over, now?"

"Yeah sure, put the coffee pot on." he said.

Carl, Sam and Nicole made quick introductions; It seemed as if Sam and Carl knew each other forever. They exchanged stories over coffee and a light lunch. There was so much to share; It would take much more time to cover all their stories. Sam retired early for the night, and Carl spent a bit more time with Nicole.

The next morning Sam was up early and, he had breakfast ready; Nicole was delighted. She did not like having breakfast alone. Most of the time, when her dad was gone, she headed to the nearest coffee shop. "So, what are your plans for today, dad?"

"Oh…., I don't know, I will just putter about and call the guys." He was not going to tell Nicole that he would spend the day with Marguerite.

Chapter Nine

Sam and Marguerite were sitting at the local restaurant when Carl and Nicole came in for lunch. They looked at each other and, walked over to them. "Hi dad" said Nicole, as she searched the looks on Marguerites face; Carl nodded and remained quiet. Sam knew he must make some introductions.

"Marguerite, this is Nicole, my daughter, and her friend, Carl. Nicole waited with Carl for Sam to explain about Marguerite accompanying him. "Oh, I'm sorry, this is my friend, Marguerite." he added.

Carl and Nicole went to a booth and waited for the waitress; They had less than an hour before they had to return to work. They ate quickly, glancing occasionally towards Sam and Marguerite.

When Nicole arrived home after work, Marguerite was at the house. She and Sam were putting finishing touches on their supper. Nicole said hello and retreated to the washroom to freshen up.

"Something smells good, what is it?" Nicole asked after she returned.

"Chicken Alfredo with Caesar Salad." replied Sam. Marguerite remained quiet.

"You must have prepared supper, Marguerite; Dad couldn't cook like this." remarked Nicole.

"Yes, I did, but your dad helped." she replied. Everyone sat and ate in silence, until Nicole popped the question; "How did you two meet?" she asked waving her fork. Sam and Marguerite looked at each other, and Sam spoke first.

"We met at a dance last year."

"You guys went to France together, and you didn't tell me!" said Nicole raising her voice.

"Nicole, said Sam, I knew you'd be upset, like now; So, I decided to wait until later to tell you."

Nicole pushed her plate aside, and she stormed off into the living room; She was angry. Marguerite and Sam looked at each other, got up and cleared the table. Then, they too retreated to the living room. "I'm sorry Nicole, I should have told you, forgive me." said Sam. Nicole still did not speak; She tossed the cushion, that she held in her lap, and stormed off to her room, angry.

"Wait until we tell her that we got married!" said Sam; Marguerite shrugged her shoulders because she did not know what to say.

The next morning, Nicole woke up to the aroma of fresh coffee, bacon and eggs. When she entered the kitchen and saw her dad standing near Marguerite, she felt so angry, stormed out the door and went to the coffee shop. She barely said hello to anybody, ate her breakfast in silence, paid the waitress and left for work.

At noon, she joined Carl for lunch, and she was still in a bad mood. "But you don't understand Carl, Dad should have told me about Marguerite!"

"Yeah, and you both would have been upset with each other when he left for France, right."

"Putting things into that perspective, you're right, only this time." she agreed. After a brief moment, Nicole invited Carl for supper. She thought it would be easier to put her anger aside by focusing on Carl.

After supper, everyone exchanged stories over coffee. And the evening flew by quickly; Carl got up to leave. "Just a minute Carl, I will walk you out to the door." said Nicole. She wanted to give him a quick kiss before he left, and express a personal thank you.

Marguerite made no move to get up, because she planned on staying for the night, again.

Somehow, Sam and Marguerite had to muster up the courage to say they were married. How and when, they did not know. "She's not saying anything about us sharing your bedroom." said Marguerite.

"I know, said Sam, perhaps she is puzzled, and does not know what to say. I know Nicole, she usually speaks her mind."

Nicole was waiting for the right opportunity to be alone with her dad. Then, she would get some answers to her nagging thoughts. "Dad, are you and Marguerite living together?"

"Yes," agreed Sam, stuttering over his words. Nicole grew quiet, as tears started to spill from her eyes. Sam reached out to her, and she gave him the cold shoulder. "Nicole, I'm telling you now, Marguerite and I are married." added Sam.

"Married, said Nicole raising her voice, what else don't I know?"

"Marguerite and I got married before we left for France. The trip was our honeymoon. I did not know how to tell you."

"Well, it's been shocking, anything else?" she questioned.

"No Nicole." said Sam; He gave her a hug and this time, she let him.

New Beginnings

Now that life at Sam's place got to be a new normal, the days were filled with happiness, some laughter and family times with Nicole and Carl. They invited Carl over quite often for supper; While Nicole and Marguerite cleaned up the dishes, Sam and Carl usually, retreated to the living room.

Just before Thanksgiving, Carl invited Nicole to a day at the park. He wanted to propose to her, and the park was the most beautiful and private place to do so. A day at the park meant long walks, a picnic and enjoying the beauty of nature. As they walked together, they became fully immersed with each other's conversation. Suddenly, Nicole tripped over a tree root; She fell forward on her knees, bracing herself with her outstretched hands. Carl was on the ground by her side in a flash. Nicole had scraped her knees and the inside of her hands and, she was making some moaning sounds.

"Let me see." said Carl as he checked her over. Then, they got up and walked over to a nearby log. "Are you ok, Nicole?" he asked as he took her hand.

"Yeah." she replied. Carl went on his knees again and searched his pockets for a ring. Nicole watched him, puzzled. Carl picked up her left hand and, held it. "Nicole, marry me?" For once, Nicole was lost for words. Carl waited briefly before she responded.

"Yes!" And they kissed and hugged each other, passionately.

"I thought you were going to ask me to go with you to New Denmark, Carl." said Nicole.

"I thought about it, but I wanted to propose first." added Carl. "Let's check into the hotel and spend a couple of nights together."

"Perhaps, we can go to New Denmark for Christmas, suggested Nicole; I had a good time last year!"

Chapter Ten

Christmas was just around the corner; There were so many things to see and do. The store windows were decorated with fir boughs, electric lights, and Christmas décor. On Friday nights and Saturday, a Santa Claus visited outside, and inside various shops, and everyone was greeting with, "Merry Christmas!"

Marguerite and Nicole decorated the inside of their home and Sam decorated the outside with Carl's help. After the decorating was finished, Marguerite and Nicole baked breads, cakes, and cookies. The aroma throughout the house was so enticing.

Days before the Christmas Holiday, Nicole and Carl was shopping for gifts for family and friends in New Denmark. As they shopped, Christmas music resonated throughout the shops. Children were gathering around Santa Claus, for a chance to tell him about their Christmas list. The spirit of Christmas was in the air.

Because Stella would worry about them, Carl and Nicole decided not to call her when they left for New Denmark. When they reached her place, her driveway was not plowed. "That's strange." said Carl.

"Do you think there's something wrong?" asked Nicole.

"Well, let's go to Neils." suggested Carl. Sure enough, that was where she was. Stella had fallen, sprained her ankle, and wrenched her back. She did not want to worry Carl, so she refrained from letting him know. Automatically, Carl was ready to give Neils a piece of his mind, but under the circumstances, he resigned from doing so.

Neils and Carla did not have their tree yet, but most of their decorating was done. Carla had baked and cleaned to no end. Stella helped with the baking, somewhat like baking tips.

"I see you don't have a tree yet, remarked Carl."

"No, we don't, replied Neils; Haven't had time."

"Well Nicole and I will get you one!"

"OK, just stay away from the neighbors' farm. I heard enough about the tree from last year."

Christmas week went by quickly. Peter, with Martha and Aaron came by often to visit, and for meals. They reminisced about old times and had a few laughs. While the men sat in the living room, the women sat in the kitchen exchanging some girl talk. Eventually everyone ended in the living room relaxing. Martha played a few Christmas songs on the piano, and everyone sang in unison. Then Martha played some Danish hymns; Stella was delighted!

The week went by quickly and, they had to say their good-byes. Despite leaving with only a few happy memories, they left with some happy and some sad emotions; They were blessed.

Chapter Eleven

It was New Year's Eve when Nicole and Carl arrived at Sam and Marguerites place. Marguerite and Sam greeted them at the front door quickly, because they had their arms full of parcels. Carl proceeded to the kitchen with the parcels, and Nicole joined her dad and Marguerite in the living room.

Marguerite and Sam anticipated hearing stories of Carl and Nicole's experiences with family and friends in New Denmark. "I'll go make us a lunch, said Marguerite, you must be hungry."

Nicole looked at Carl, and then she said, "Yes we are, most places were closed and, we were anxious to get home. Is there any Tourtiere left?" she asked as she searched the fridge; Tourtiere was Nicole's favorite.

Nicole and Carl were totally exhausted. "Carl, stay the night with us; Tomorrow is New Year's after all." said Nicole. Before Carl could say yes, Sam agreed with Nicole.

"You can sleep in the guest room." said Marguerite.

Nicole slept in the next morning, but Carl got up early. Perhaps, it was the smell of fresh coffee, bacon and eggs. "Good morning Carl, said Marguerite and Sam in unison, did you sleep well?"

"Yes, I fell asleep, when my head touched the pillow." he answered. Marguerite served Carl and Sam their breakfast, and just when she was ready to prepare her plate, Nicole came in. She looked a big groggy still, and she poured herself a cup of coffee. Marguerite was ready to serve her breakfast, but she declined the offer. After breakfast Sam and Carl took a coffee to the living room. They had lots to talk about, and the ladies stayed in the kitchen. They, too, had lots to talk about.

Now, with Christmas and New Years behind them, Nicole and Carl started plans for their wedding. June first was their proposed date; And, after their wedding ceremony, they planned on having their honeymoon in Hawaii. They could not come to an agreement, however, about where they would get married. "I want to get married in our church, here in Toronto." said Nicole.

"And I'm sorry, we must get married in New Denmark." said Carl.

"Well, the bride always gets her choice according to wedding rules." added Nicole.

"Rules can be broken; I say we get married in New Denmark." added Carl.

"Eww Carl, you are so stubborn!" exclaimed Nicole putting her hands in the air.

Carl tried to get her to understand that his mom could not make the trip to Toronto. Still, Nicole was adamant about where she wanted her wedding to take place.

"Why don't we elope? teased Carl, then we can have our wedding and honeymoon together." Nicole just glared at Carl, and she did not say anything.

After pondering over the thought of eloping, Nicole started to like the idea. It would certainly resolve a lot of issues.

CHAPTER TWELVE

Nicole and Carl were on a plane, leaving Toronto International Airport and soon, they were arriving in Hawaii. They were greeted by island people, welcoming them and putting leis around their neck. It was warm, but, a slight breeze touched their skin, as they walked away from the plane. A steward came, took their luggage, and drove them to their seaside cottage, a few minutes away.

"Oh Carl, this is beautiful!" exclaimed Nicole as she flopped on the lofty bed. Carl joined her, said nothing, and kissed her so passionately. Nicole responded, and their pleasure of the moment, continued more.

They relaxed into the early evening, and then, they walked to an open restaurant. The menu was lavished with fresh fruit, and tropical drinks. Hawaiian music played softly; The waiter brought a cold bottle of wine in a bucket of crushed ice before he took their order.

"So, what are you having, Nicole?"

"I'm not sure, she replied still looking at the menu, chicken salad for now."

"I'm having the seafood plate; It looks delicious." said Carl. They both were afraid to order something out of the ordinary.

After, they went for a walk on a beach of white-colored sand and palm trees nearby, swaying in a gentle breeze. "Are we in heaven, Carl? asked Nicole.

"Close to it, Nicole." he said, wrapping his arm around her waist. They walked in their bare feet, until it was nearly dark. They kissed, and then, they returned to their cabin.

"I'm glad we eloped, Carl; I didn't realize how heavenly this could be!" she said before she started to kiss him more, and more, and more………

The next morning, they woke up to sunshine, and tropical birds singing. They showered and walked to the same restaurant that, they had been to the night before. Everything looked so delectable, again with fresh fruit and tropical juices. "Is bacon and eggs on the menu?" asked Carl.

"Sure, we can accommodate you, said the waiter……. and, for the beautiful lady?"

"I'll have the same." added Nicole.

After breakfast, they toured the island; There was so much to see and do. Next on their agenda, they had to find a local priest. They walked to an open market. "Where can we find a priest?" asked Carl.

"Take a ride with the guy in the Jeep, said a man. He will help you."

They drove a short distance to a building with a thatched roof. There was a cross on the roof to identify the place. They proceeded inside, and they did not see anybody at first. "Hello," said a man wearing a collar. "How can I help you?" said the priest.

Carl spoke first, "We want to get married." Carl looked at Nicole and, they exchanged a quick kiss.

"Oh!," said the priest, speaking with a strong accent. "Come sit, he said, let's get your information and, then we can arrange your wedding."

Chapter Thirteen

Carl stood with the priest, waiting for Nicole; A strange man stood beside him. He was obviously the best man and, the maid of honor was with Nicole, assisting her. Carl was dressed in an ivory-colored silk shirt opened to his chest. He wore white trousers with the hems rolled up, exposing bare legs and bare feet.

The maid of honor walked before Nicole, giving sufficient time for Nicole to walk solo to her place. Nicole was breath-taking in her silk gown. The gown was ivory-colored, and form-fitting. The cowl neckline dipped below her bust. And slits from the hem of the gown revealed her slender, and tanned legs. Her bouquet consisted of a few white orchids, with a bit of greenery, tied with pale pink ribbons. She was also bare feet.

The ceremony lasted for a short time. After they exchanged their vows, they walked to an open platform, where live Hawaiian music played. Everyone danced and dined into the night. Then, they walked together, holding hands, back to their cottage. There, they expressed their love and happiness to each other. They kissed passionately, and then with a glass of wine they toasted to each other. "Congratulations, Mrs. Nicole Larsen."

"And congratulations, Mr. Carl Larsen!"

Their two weeks stay in Hawaii was soon over and, they would be returning to Toronto. They took in their last days touring the island, shopped for gifts, and took long walks on the beach. The day arrived to return home; They said their goodbyes and, boarded the plane, back to Toronto.

Upon their arrival at the Toronto International Airport, they were met by Sam and Marguerite. They hugged each other and then, they got into the car and headed to Carl's place.

Sam and Marguerite did not visit long, because they knew Nicole and Carl were exhausted.

They slept in until almost noon the next day. They took a quick shower together and, proceeded to have brunch. Carl made the coffee while Nicole got the bacon and eggs ready. They ate, buffet style and toasted to each other with their orange juice, and they exchanged more kisses. They were beyond happy.

After brunch, Carl called his mom. "Carl, I am surprised, are you and Nicole home?" answered Stella.

"Yes mom, Nicole is right beside me, do you want to talk to her?"

"Ya, sure." said Stella. Sam passed the phone to Nicole; Stella's voice started to tremble, so Nicole passed the phone back to Carl.

"Mom, we'll call again soon, said Carl; Bye mom." he added as he hung up.

Stella must have said, "I love you Carl," because Carl had to keep back his tears.

Carl and Nicole took another coffee, sat down in the living room, and they called Marguerite and Sam. Sam answered the phone.

"Hello, said Sam with a French accent; Marguerite, Nicole's on the phone, come!" Marguerite came and sat next to Sam on the sofa.

"Carl and I are having a bar-b-que tonight. We want you and Marguerite to come over." suggested Nicole. Sam reiterated everything to Marguerite and asked her if she wanted to go.

"Well, of course, she said, what time?"

Chapter Fourteen

It was the end of June; Nicole and Carl were on their way to New Denmark. They were excited about visiting with Stella, Neils and Peter, and their families. They were looking forward to sharing their experiences regarding their wedding in Hawaii.

"Yes mom, the beaches were beautiful; The sand was white and warm. Sometimes, it even sparkled." said Carl.

"Do you have some pictures with you?" asked Stella.

"Yeah mom, we do." Grab that bag, Nicole, I put some pictures in it." said Carl. Nicole found the pictures, and she went to sit on the other side of Stella, as they looked at the pictures together.

"Oh my, exclaimed Stella as she looked at the wedding pictures, beautiful, can I have this one to keep?" she asked, while tears blurred her vision.

"Yes mom, this one is yours!" said Carl, and he handed the picture to her.

The next day, Nicole helped Stella with meals and housework. They were inviting Peter, Neils and family over for supper. It was easier to have everybody over, rather than going to each separate home. And, it was nice for Stella, having her family all together, like a family reunion. It was the best opportunity to give the gifts they purchased in Hawaii, besides the photos.

"Uncle Carl, I'd like to go to Hawaii sometime." said Aaron.

"Perhaps, you will someday, save up your money, Aaron." replied Carl.

"But that will take a long time, for me." added Aaron.

Carl reached into his pocket, retrieved a fifty-dollar bill, and handed it to him.

"Thanks, Uncle Carl!" He was ecstatic and, he stashed the money into his pocket.

On Monday morning, Nicole and Carl were saying goodbye, and leaving for their long drive back to Toronto. They had a wonderful visit.

Chapter Fifteen

Nicole hurried off to the washroom of New Market Realty; She felt like vomiting. She had eaten something that was not agreeing with her, or......she was pregnant! She was going to the medical clinic after work. Sure enough, the test results showed positively pregnant. She was thrilled, but she thought, "How would Carl react?"

Before supper, Nicole told Carl the news. He was so excited, he picked Nicole up of her feet, and kissed her.

"So, when is the due date, Nicole?" asked Carl.

"Sometime, around the end of April." she answered.

"Well tonight, we are going out to celebrate, said Carl; I'm so excited!"

The morning sickness continued, month after month and Nicole visited her family doctor on a regular basis. The doctor said it was normal to experience so much sickness. He prescribed some vitamins, and he reassured her, she and the baby were fine.

"Ah………cried out Nicole early one morning; Again, she cried Ah………; Carl heard her.

"What's the matter?" he asked. Nicole could not respond, because of the pain, and she held on to her abdomen. Carl grabbed his car keys, went out the door, and drove the car as close as he could to the front door. He opened the passenger door and then, he went to the front door of the house and, left it open. He walked over to Nicole, picked her up and, he carried her to the car. She was still experiencing a lot of pain. Carl drove to the hospital, as fast as he could and, he pulled up close to the hospital. He opened the emergency doors of the hospital, grabbed a wheelchair and, went back for Nicole. A nurse stood waiting for them at the door. More staff came and, they brought Nicole into a room for an assessment. Then, they quickly brought her to a delivery room. An hour passed, then a few more. Carl was feeling panicky and scared. Every time he saw a nurse, he reached out to her, and he asked about Nicole. "Is my wife, ok?"

"Sorry, sir, I don't know." they replied most of the time.

Finally, Carl saw the Doctor come out of the delivery room, looking so discouraged and shaking his head. Carl was afraid to ask, "How's Nicole?"

The doctor looked away from Carl and then, he turned to tell him, "Nicole will be ok."

"And the baby." continued Carl.

The doctor shook his head and, did not say anything.

"What about the baby?" Carl persisted to ask.

"He didn't make it." said the doctor, finally.

"The baby was a boy, you said he." reiterated Carl. The doctor put a hand on Carl's shoulder, said "yes." and then he walked away.

Carl feared facing Nicole. He was experiencing one of the most horrible and heartbreaking times of his life; Nicole was experiencing the same. Carl called Sam and Marguerite. "I haven't spoken to Nicole yet Sam, said Carl; I don't know what to say."

"Get in there, now Carl, before……."; Sam did not finish saying what he wanted.

Carl walked to Nicole's room and stood by the door, briefly before he entered the room. Nicole appeared to be asleep but, she was not. She kept her back turned away from the door and, she laid there staring a blank stare.

"Nicole." said Carl. She did not respond and, she continued to lie in the same position. Carl walked around the bed so he could speak to her, again. She rolled over on her other side. Carl told her, he was leaving but, he would return. He told her that he called her dad and Marguerite and, updated them about everything. Now, Carl could not see the tears that were running down Nicole's cheeks.

Carl had so many decisions to make and, he did not know where to start. He buried his head in his hands and, he started to pray, like never before in his life. "Please, forgive me Lord for my sins. I beg you for your help; I will do whatever it takes, just help me."

Carl felt some of the weight of remorse lifting after praying and, he was now regaining some inner strength. God was answering his prayers; He just needed some faith.

He went to get some red roses for Nicole and then, he headed to the hospital. Nicole was sitting in a wheelchair in the foyer. She looked up when she saw him and, she smiled, just a little smile. He handed her the roses; She took them and laid them on her lap. "I'm so sorry Nicole, about everything; We will get through this somehow." Nicole looked at him and she began sobbing, relentlessly. Carl kissed her on the head, and then, with a soft voice, he pleaded, "Our baby needs a name, do you have one in mind?"

"Yes, Isaac, his name is Isaac." Nicole replied.

"And, Nicole, we need to sign his Birth Certificate, and his Death Certificate."

Carl was surprised that Nicole complied with all the requirements necessary without any fuss.

"Nicole, said Carl, I prayed to God this morning." Nicole looked at him, and she gave another little smile and, Carl wheeled Nicole over to the nurses' station; And, they signed the papers. God had given them his peace.

Chapter Sixteen

"After five days in the hospital, Nicole came home. Carl had taken a month off from work earlier, and now, he had three weeks left. Nicole needed a lot of assistance with the chores and her daily routine; Therefore, Carl hired a caregiver for the next month.

Nicole was experiencing depression, and without a doubt, she was suffering post-partum issues, also. The hospital provided much needed emotional support, and both Carl and Nicole benefited from the program.

In May, they held a memorial for Baby Isaac; Sam and Marguerite joined them at the cemetery. It was a very emotional ceremony, and they all stood arm in arm with each other, for much needed support. After the service, they went to the local restaurant for dinner. Nicole had not been getting out, so it was a good opportunity to join the parents for a meal, away from home.

"Carl, you're going back to work." said Nicole.

"Yeah, Jack called, and he expects me back on site on Monday." answered Carl.

"What happens if I need you?" asked Nicole. She was nervous about Carl going back to work, and she kept wondering, what if?

Carl reminded her about her caregiver, looked at her in the eyes and said, "Nicole, it will be good to gain your independence again."

When Carl arrived on the work site, on Monday morning, his boss called him into the trailer. "Carl, we had some changes made since you left." Carl looked at Jack and waited for him to say more. "Our Company, Toronto Northern Construction has gone Union."

"And so, what is happening?' asked Carl.

"We hired a licensed carpenter, James Butler. He will be our foreman; We will work as a team." added Jack.

"And, where does that leave me?" asked Carl.

"Your job will continue the same as usual, however, you and the others will have to take courses to become certified. The other guys have already started their course." added Jack.

There were other changes happening regarding Carl's job. The wages were being adjusted accordingly to a seniority list. Now, Carl figured, he was the lowest on the list. Carl understood the changes were bound to happen, sooner or later; However, he didn't anticipate the competition that changed the working morale. But it did!

Chapter Seventeen

"Carl, I'm going back to work." said Nicole, one evening while they were enjoying a television program together. Carl was delighted to hear Nicole saying so, however, he tried not to show his feelings. "Well, what do you think?" she asked.

"It's up to you; I think it's a good idea." he replied.

Nicole's Company, New Market Realty was experiencing a decline in sales, however, it was still holding its own. Nicole brought new incentives and a breath of fresh air with her return. Everyone dug in their heels, and shortly, sales started to escalate; "Wow, I like your advertisement, "New to You, Sally!" said Nicole.

Sally looked up from her computer and said, "Thank you, Nicole; I'm so glad you are back."

Nicole's spirits were lifting; She enjoyed her job again, and she anticipated the start of each new day. She looked forward to spending time with friends and her parents, so she got on the phone.

"Hello dad, Carl and I are having friends over on Saturday for a barbeque. We would be happy having you and Marguerite over, like old times."

"Sure, I will let Marguerite know, said Sam; She loves a party."

Marguerite called Nicole back; "Your dad and I would like to help with the party, she said; You know how we like working together with you and Carl."

"Yeah, I do too; And thanks, Marguerite." said Nicole.

The party continued from supper into the evening; Everyone was having a good time telling stories and having a few good laughs. That night Carl and Nicole made love and basked in their love until they fell asleep. They would later find out, that Nicole was pregnant, again.

It took nearly two months before Nicole realized that she was having another baby. "Carl, I'm scared; I need a hug, right now." she said. Carl hugged Nicole; He was scared, too, but he had to be brave, and not say so.

Nicole experienced some morning sickness at first, but it subsided after her fifth month; She was able to continue working until her eighth month, without complications this time.

Nicole started to get twinges of pain in her lower back throughout the day. Carl noticed that Nicole was flinching occasionally, that evening. "Nicole are you ok?" he asked.

"I keep getting these pains in my back." she said.

"Well, get ready, I'm taking you to the hospital." said Carl.

"But Carl, the doctor said……."; She did not get to finish what she was going to say.

"Come on, Nicole, we're going to the hospital now!" insisted Carl.

Nicole was in labor for nine hours, before the nurse took her to the delivery room. Her labor pains were increasing greatly, and her water broke. The baby was ready to make his or her way into the world. Then, the baby cried good and loud. "A girl, it's a girl" said the doctor as he laid the baby on Nicole's abdomen.

"Is she ok?" asked Nicole, as she kept touching her baby.

"Yes, she is!" said the doctor. He cut the baby's cord and placed the baby into Nicole's waiting arms.

Carl was just outside the door; He heard the baby cry, and he looked upward, and he said, "Thank you Jesus." He had been praying fervently.

The door opened; The doctor was beaming with the biggest smile. "You can go in!" he said. Carl went in and walked over to Nicole and placed a kiss on her head. "A baby girl Carl, we got a baby girl!" said Nicole. Carl opened the blanket and peered at their tiny miracle. He touched her cheek, ever so gently. "I love you, Nicole!" he said.

Nicole responded with, "I love you too!"

A nurse came in to get the baby and Carl left, but not before he gave Nicole another kiss.

Carl went straight to Sam's place to tell him and Marguerite about the baby. He was so excited; Usually, he rang the doorbell, but today, he walked straight in. Sam and Marguerite were having breakfast. They looked at Carl, and they were speechless. "We have a baby, a baby girl!" he said.

"How's Nicole?" questioned Sam.

"She's fine, I'm going back later; 'Gotta get some flowers, and we gotta give that baby a name!" said Carl.

Sam and Marguerite wanted to know all the details about Nicole and the baby. Carl answered all their questions, before he left to go home; Sam and Marguerite were going to visit Nicole in the afternoon.

Carl went home and had a little sleep; He was exhausted!

Carl and Nicole had discussed about selecting baby names a bit earlier. A boy would be called Samuel, and a girl would be Marianne. So, Marianne came first; Possibly, Sam will come next.

Shortly after having the baby, Nicole experienced post-partum depression. Marianne kept Nicole up all hours of the night; It seemed as if Marianne slept better during the day.

Carl felt helpless, because Nicole was breast feeding; Sometimes, she fell asleep while she was feeding the baby.

Carl hired a housekeeper; At least, that would alleviate some of Nicole's responsibilities.

Soon, Marianne was smiling, and she was becoming a real delight. By the time she turned five months old, Nicole weaned her from breast feeding. Nicole planned on returning to work; They were becoming financially strapped and besides, Nicole wanted to get back to her Real-estate Company.

With more independence, and more money, Carl and Nicole were able to spend more time for themselves, friends and for Sam and Marguerite.

Marianne was forever growing, and her needs were forever changing. Carl and Nicole loved to shop for her and, Sam and Marguerite were always buying new clothes and new toys, as well.

Chapter Eighteen

"Hello, Nicole, Marguerite was calling, come quick, it's your dad." she said.

Nicole did not waste any time. "Carl, Carl, something is wrong with dad, hurry!" said Nicole.

"I'll stay with Marianne, you go!" blurted out Carl; He was afraid.

Nicole hurried to Sam's place; She burst inside to the living room. Marguerite was beside Sam, sitting on the sofa. Sam was having chest pains on his left side, and he could not lie down. "I'm calling the ambulance right now!" said Nicole.

"I don't want an ambulance Nicole, just take me to the hospital!" cried Sam. He was experiencing a lot of pain, so he spoke sharply.

To prepare the staff in the Emergency Department at the hospital, Nicole gave them a quick call. Then she helped her dad to the car; Marguerite went with them.

An orderly was waiting at the door when they arrived. He helped Sam into a wheelchair, and he hurried off to the Emergency with him. Marguerite followed the orderly, and Nicole stopped at the desk to register her dad.

A nurse hooked up a heart monitor, and she attached an IV to Sam's arm; Then, the doctor came in, and he began assessing Sam's vitals.

Marguerite was directed to a waiting room, and Nicole joined her there. "Are you ok, Marguerite?" asked Nicole.

"Yes, I'm ok." she said, despite the fact, her hands were trembling.

Forty minutes later, the doctor had completed his initial assessment; He found Nicole and Marguerite in the waiting room.

"I don't think Sam took a heart attack; I'm keeping him in overnight, and I should know more by tomorrow." said the doctor.

Marguerite and Nicole were relieved to hear that Sam did not have a heart attack, and they left for home.

After arriving at Marguerite's place, Nicole had Marguerite pack an overnight bag, because she was spending the night with her.

"Na, Na" said Marianne, when she saw her grandmother the next morning. Marguerite picked her up and gave her a big bear hug.

"Breakfast is ready Marguerite, said Carl; Nicole is waiting for us in the kitchen."

The kitchen smelled of bacon, eggs and coffee, and Nicole was serving breakfast, buffet style. "Marguerite, we'll go see dad around one o'clock, Is that ok with you?" asked Nicole.

"Sure, that will give me time to spend with Marianne; They should have some answers regarding Sam, by then." added Marguerite.

"Na, Na," said Marianne, as she crawled over to her grandmother, again. This time, she had her favorite blanket, and she reached up for her grandmother to pick her up. Marguerite picked her up and carried her over to a rocking chair. There, they sat and rocked until Marianne fell asleep.

Carl came into the room, and he saw that Marianne had fallen asleep. He took her from Marguerite and carried her to her room. He laid her in her crib, and tucked her blanket beside her face, ever so gently.

Chapter Nineteen

Nicole and Marguerite went to the Nurses Station; "Could we visit with Samuel Lemieux?"

"Yes, replied the nurse, he's in room 18, down the hall on your left."

Nicole peeked in the door, first, then she whispered to Marguerite, "He's awake!" before they entered the room.

"Ah, my two favorite gals! said Sam, come in, come in!"

Marguerite gave Sam a quick kiss on his forehead first, then Nicole, likewise. "How are you feeling, today, dad; Is the pain gone?" asked Nicole. Marguerite listened intently, while Sam explained that he did not have a heart attack.

"I have a hiatus hernia, and that is what caused the pain."

"Well, is that dangerous?" asked Marguerite.

"It can be, sometime; The doctor gave me some information, and a diet," explained Sam.

"When can you come home, dad?" asked Nicole.

"The doctor is coming in at two to see me, and I can go home after." said Sam.

Carl heard the car pull up the driveway; He waited at the door for Nicole. He was anxious to get an update on Sam. "So, how was Sam feeling today?" he asked.

"He's home; I took dad and Marguerite home a few minutes ago." Nicole replied and gave Carl a quick kiss.

"I'm hungry, said Carl, let's take Marianne and go out for supper."

"Sure, said Nicole; Is Marianne awake?" she asked.

"Yes, and I have her all dressed up; I was hoping you'd want to go out!" added Carl.

"Let's go to the Chinese Buffet, suggested Nicole, it'll be good for a change."

A waitress got a highchair for Marianne; And, Marianne began to make a fuss as Carl started to secure her in it. "Usually, she is fine in a highchair." expressed Carl and, he took her out of it. Nicole took her from Carl, and then she put her back into the chair. She did not secure her, and Marianne was fine.

"You see, I have a magic touch!" said Nicole.

"Whatever works, right." said Carl.

Marianne fell asleep, as usual, while they drove home. Carl carried her inside, and Nicole got her changed into her PJ's, and together, they tucked her into her crib. After, they called Marguerite and Sam. Marguerite picked up the phone quickly because Sam was asleep. "Hello," she whispered into the phone.

"It is me, Nicole said, how is dad doing?"

"He's asleep right now." Marguerite started to say, just as Sam asked, "Who is on the phone?"

"It's Nicole, said Marguerite, would you like to speak to her?"

"Yes, please." said Sam as he reached for the phone. "Yes, Nicole, I'm fine; Will be better after a night in my own bed."

"Have a good night dad, and tell Marguerite the same, expressed Nicole; I love you dad."

"I love you too Nicole!" added Sam.

Chapter Twenty

Thanksgiving weekend was just around the corner and, Carl was hoping to go to New Denmark for the long weekend. Marianne was now, more than seven months old, and Carl's family had never seen her yet. Carl kept in touch with his mom by mail, and he sent loads of pictures.

"I want my mom to see Marianne, Nicole; Could we take the trip to New Denmark this weekend?" suggested Carl.

"You're right, Carl; Can we leave right after work?" asked Nicole. Carl was surprised that Nicole didn't hesitate about going to New Denmark, this time.

"I can't wait to see mom's face when she sees Marianne!" said Carl. "Did you bring the camera, Nicole?" asked Carl.

"It's right here, ready to go!" replied Nicole.

Stella's face lit up when she opened her door, seeing Carl, Nicole and Marianne. Nicole was ready with the camera, snapped a picture, and followed everyone inside.

"Come in, come in, welcomed Stella. have a seat, you must be tired."

Just when Stella reached out to pick Marianne up, she began crying; And, she clung to her mother.

"Don't feel bad Stella, she will warm up to you soon." said Nicole.

"Yeah, said Carl; Just ignore her."

It was nine o'clock in the morning, and nobody had breakfast yet. Marianne helped Stella in the kitchen, preparing breakfast while Carl occupied Marianne. Soon the aroma of bacon, eggs and coffee filled the entire house.

"So, what's your agenda for today, mom?" asked Carl.

"Oh, I don't know." replied Stella.

"Do you want Peter and Neils to come and visit after supper?" asked Carl.

"Yes, it would be like old times." added Stella.

Nicole and Stella puttered about the house getting everything cleaned up, while Carl checked out his mother's shed and the yard.

Peter, Martha and Aaron arrived at seven; Neils and his family arrived a few minutes later. Everyone sat in the living room, talking and exchanging the latest events. Marianne was making herself home now, and she crawled right over to Aaron. Aaron reached out to her, "Wanna come?" he asked. She lifted a hand, and Aaron picked her up; Everyone awed over Aaron and Marianne.

"He must have the magic touch." said Carl.

The conversations circled around Marianne and Stella. "Did you bring some pictures of Marianne with you?" asked Martha.

"We sure did; Stella and I went through them all today; They are right here on the coffee table." said Nicole.

"Ohhh Nicole, I love this one, can I keep it?" asked Martha.

"Let me see, added Nicole; Yes sure, you can keep it; I wanted to make sure it wasn't promised to Stella."

Stella looked up; She was pleased that Nicole let her have first choice with the pictures.

Carl changed the subject, "Now Mom, you will need your roof repaired soon, some of the shingles seem to be loose; And there are a few other things that need to be done around the house.

"What do I say, Carl?" asked Stella.

"I say, I will assess the needed repairs, and I will hire someone to do the job." remarked Carl.

"But Carl", Stella started to say something, and Carl stopped her.

"Mom, I am making plans to have the work done, starting when Nicole and I leave. No buts!"

"Before everyone leaves, let's have a lunch." suggested Stella. The ladies proceeded to help Stella in the kitchen, and the men remained in the living room. Aaron continued to entertain Marianne.

Chapter Twenty-One

It was late when everyone got home in Toronto. Despite the fact, Nicole and Carl shared the driving, they were tired; Even Marianne was cranky. The house was not warm and inviting when they went inside, so Carl started a fire in the fireplace. Nicole got Marianne changed into a warm sleeper, and then they joined Carl in the living room. "Come see dad!" said Carl as he reached toward Marianne. She went to her dad willingly, and Nicole decided she, too, would get changed into some warm and snuggly night clothes.

While Carl rocked with Marianne near the fireplace, she fell fast asleep. When Nicole came back to the living room, she retrieved her camera from her shoulder bag, and she took a lasting memory picture.

Together Carl and Nicole went to Marianne's room, and they tucked her in. They looked at each other, longingly, and they gave each other a kiss before they left her room. The rest of the evening was theirs.

The following Tuesday, everyone was back to work. Carl and Nicole met at their usual restaurant for lunch. Their trip to New Denmark had made a positive impact on them; They both were feeling a lightness, in their spirit since their trip.

After supper, Nicole called her dad and Marguerite; Carl sat right next to Nicole. "Hi Dad, how are you and Marguerite doing?" she asked.

"Great, Sam replied, how was your trip?" Sam was asking so many questions, therefore, Nicole whispered to Carl, "Let's invite dad and Marguerite over for supper tomorrow night."

The next night, Marguerite and Sam arrived a bit early; They were anxious to catch up on Nicole and Carls' trip to New Denmark. Marguerite baked an apple pie, Carls' favorite.

"I wasn't expecting an apple pie said Nicole but, thank you." Marguerite and Nicole went into the kitchen to check on supper, lasagne, baked potatoes, and homemade bread; Mmmm, that all smells so good." said Marguerite.

Marianne was sitting in her highchair, and when she saw Marguerite, she started motions with her hands, saying "Ga, Ga". She could not say Grammie yet, though she tried.

"Can I take her?" asked Marguerite.

"You sure can." answered Nicole.

Marguerite carried Marianne into the living room, "Look who I got!" she said as she walked over to Sam. Sam reached out to Marianne, and she let her grandfather take her.

Soon Nicole came into the living room, "Supper is ready, she said, we're eating buffet style tonight."

Everyone had a delightful evening together. Sam and Carl had a great time talking over coffee in the living room, while Nicole, Marguerite and Marianne enjoyed some girls' talk in the kitchen.

Before Sam and Marguerite left, Marguerite got Marianne into her pj's and carried her to her grandfather to say Goodbyes. "Kisses, Marianne." said Sam, as he kissed her on her forehead.

Marianne surprised everyone by blowing kisses; Carl had been trying to teach her how.

"Oh, you are just so precious!" said Marguerite, as she took Marianne's little hand, just as they were leaving.

"It was so nice Carl, having Dad and Marguerite in for supper." said Nicole.

"Yes Nicole, I had a great evening. Carl and Nicole gave each other a hug and then, they got ready for bed.

Chapter Twenty-Two

Nicole invited Marguerite out for a girls' night. They needed to do some Christmas shopping for their men; And they had to make plans for Christmas decorating and baking. And a girl's night out was on their agenda for the evening; Carl and Sam were babysitting.

They shopped at the local department store, and when they got tired of shopping, they headed to the family restaurant.

The outside and the inside of the restaurant was decorated with fir wreaths, swags and electric lights. It not only looked festive, but it smelled like Christmas. Nicole found a cozy booth, and they soon had a waitress dressed in Christmas attire, waiting on them.

"I'll have a piece of hot apple pie, with butterscotch ripple ice-cream; Then, I'll have a glass of eggnog to drink." said Nicole.

"I'll have the same, except I'll have a cup of tea with mine." said Marguerite.

While they ate their pie, they discussed plans for the holiday; Like baking, decorating, and exchanging gift ideas.

"Marguerite, I'm buying Carl, a new pick-up for Christmas; He really needs one!" said Nicole.

"Wow, a pick-up, that's a big gift, exclaimed Marguerite; How are you going to hide that from him?"

"I got it all figured out, we'll park it behind your house! said Nicole; On Christmas eve, you and dad can drive it to our place, before Mass."

"We must be going to Mass, on Christmas eve." suggested Marguerite.

"Yes, that's the plan, said Nicole; I'm telling Carl, soon."

"What about Marianne?" questioned Marguerite.

"Between you and dad, Carl and I, we should be able to look after her." suggested Nicole.

Then, Nicole looked at her watch. It was 9:50 pm; We better get home!"

"Yeah, before those men get worried about us; Marianne should be asleep, no?" added Marguerite.

The men were starting to get a bit worried, however, they did not want to say so, when their wives got home. "So, you ladies had a good time, right!" said Carl. Sam stood quietly while awaiting their responses.

"Yes, we did, and how was your evening with Marianne?" asked Nicole.

"Perfect." said Carl and Sam in unison. "Well, she did ask about her Grammy, and her mom, before she went to bed." added Sam.

"Yeah." added Carl.

"Thanks Dad, for helping Carl to babysit, we'll have to do this more often." suggested Nicole.

Everyone looked at each other, after Nicole's remark, with big grins on their face.

Nicole went to Marguerites' place for the next two weekends to help with the Christmas baking. They baked everything from cookies, breads, pies, including their famous Tourtiere.

While Nicole and Marguerite baked, the men baby-sat Marianne. The first Saturday, the guys went shopping for a couple of Christmas trees. Marianne was delighted over seeing so many children at the department store, grocery store and even the hardware store.

Santa Claus was at the Department Store, and Kids were lined up, like you would not believe. Marianne was all smiles, while she waited in line with her dad and grampie for her turn to see Santa. But, when Carl passed her over to Santa, she started to scream and cry; She was scared! Children stared and continued, however, on their way toward Santa.

"Carl, we have to go to Christmas eve Mass." said Nicole when she got home that evening.

"Why?" responded Carl with a wondering look on his face.

"Because Dad and Marguerite are going to pick us up at eleven o'clock Christmas Eve." said Nicole.

"And, what about Marianne?" questioned Carl.

"We're bringing her with us." responded Nicole.

"So, Christmas Eve, sounds like a plan." added Carl.

Carl had no idea that Marguerite and Sam were coming to their place with his new Pick-up. Nicole was so excited; She could hardly wait until her dad and Marguerite would arrive. She turned on the yard light, so they could easily see the pick-up.

Marguerite and Sam arrived a bit early; Carl answered the door, and then he saw the new pick-up that Sam and Marguerite arrived in.

"You guys' are driving in style; Did you get a new Pick-up?" he asked.

"Yeah, we did!" said Sam, as he and Marguerite went inside. They stood by the door, and Sam passed the keys to Carl, saying, "Merry Christmas, Carl!"

Carl's mouth flew open in surprise. He did not know what to say, and Sam explained, "It's your Christmas present from Nicole; Let's go outside and check it out." said Sam.

Chapter Twenty-Three

It was wonderful experiencing Christmas celebrations with Sam, Marguerite and Marianne. Marianne did not understand all the excitement about everything however, she loved all the undivided attention that she was getting. She performed on queue with each opportunity, despite her sleep time was disrupted by the Mass Service.

"Celebrating Mass was special, I'm glad we went, said Carl; Is anybody hungry?"

"I am, said Sam; Come on girls, where is all that good food?"

"Tourtiere, everybody?" asked Nicole.

"Tourtiere and apple pie for dessert?" added Marguerite.

After everyone had eaten, they left the table and headed straight to the Christmas tree. Sam carried Marianne, and everyone stared with awe over the site of gifts under the tree.

New Beginnings

Carl passed the gifts out to everyone, one by one. Marianne came first, of course; Next was Nicole.

"Oh Carl, it's beautiful! Nicole exclaimed as she flashed the diamond ring around. Thanks Carl, I love it!" she exclaimed and then, she gave Carl a quick kiss.

"Mom and dad, this is yours together from all of us!" said Carl as he passed them their gifts.

"Hurry up, Marguerite, you're taking too long!" said Sam.

"Oh, you guys!" said Marguerite. Sam was speechless as they admired the family portrait.

"Mom, dad, open the big gift, now said Nicole; You'll love it."

"Come Marianne, said Sam, help us, like this!" Sam took Marianne's little hands, and together they opened the big box.

"A record player!" exclaimed Marguerite and Sam in unison. And two records! added Sam.

"Can we play a record, now?" asked Sam.

"Sure." said Carl. Together Carl and Sam had the record player running. They danced with Marianne to the tunes of Bing Crosby, while Nicole and Marguerite cleaned up the dishes.

Chapter Twenty-Four

Marianne was five years old before Nicole had baby Sam, their dream come true. Sam was the most passive baby, and only became demanding when his needs were not met. Nicole still, however experienced the baby blues. Perhaps, because she knew that there wouldn't be any more babies due to complications during delivery of Sam.

"Mommy wake up, mommy, baby Sam is crying." said Marianne as she crawled into bed with her mother. Carl had already gone to work, otherwise, he would have tended to the children.

Nicole was really struggling with facing the day. "Oh Marianne, we better go see Sam; Will you help mommy, please?" asked Nicole.

"K, mommy." said Marianne as she ran into baby Sam's room.

New Beginnings

When Carl came home, Marianne raced to the door to welcome her dad. "Dad, Dad, see my new shoes!" she said as she flopped on the floor and lifted a foot.

"New shoes, nice; Did mommy buy them?" he asked.

"No, Grammy did." she replied.

Nicole came to the door holding baby Sam on her hips. Carl could see that the baby had been crying. He gave Nicole a quick kiss and, picked up Marianne before he went into the kitchen. Dishes filled the sink, and the floors were sticky. Nicole followed Carl into the kitchen, still holding the baby on her hip.

Instead of getting angry at Nicole for neglecting her responsibilities, he empathized with her. He put Marianne in her highchair, then he took Sam from Nicole and put him in his carriage by the kitchen table. He gave Nicole a long hug that she really needed. "Come on, Sweetie, lets get some supper."

Nicole started to cry. Carl turned to her and hugged her some more.

"No cry, mommy!" said Marianne.

Nicole walked over to Marianne, kissed her on the head and then, proceeded to help Carl with supper.

After supper, Carl helped Nicole clear the table and wash the dishes. Then, they gave both Marianne and Sam a bath, together. "Daddy, look at me, said Marianne, I can swim." as she splashed around in the tub getting everyone wet. Everyone was laughing, except for baby Sam; He was rather annoyed by it all.

After their bath, Carl and Nicole dressed them in their pj's and brought them into the living room in front of the cozy fireplace. Nicole held Sam, and fed him his formula, while Carl read Marianne a bedtime story.

After the children were nicely tucked into their bed, Nicole and Carl was more than ready for their quiet time.

Chapter Twenty-Five

Nicole returned to work, when baby Sam was six months old. Her depression had lifted, and her Company needed her back in the office. She worked from home as much as she could, however, the staff needed her often, at the spur of the moment sometimes.

"Nicole, someone wants you to visit their property asap; I'll, finish your project." said Lillian.

"Nicole, we need that ad in the paper before next week." said another worker.

Nicole was indispensable; She wondered how they managed without her by their side.

Work occupied most of Carl and Nicole's time, however, their free time was spent with their children, and Marguerite and Sam.

They took family vacations, and many trips to New Denmark, New Brunswick to visit Stella. She was slowing down, but thank God, she could still stay in her home, and entertain her friends and family.

Aaron's graduation was a month away, and Stella was cleaning her house and baking up a storm. She was never one to procrastinate about anything.

"Mom, slow down." said Carl over the phone; "We are coming home to help you."

"I know, I'm so excited!" added Stella.

When Carl and Nicole arrived in New Denmark with the children, they noticed that Stella looked tired, but they didn't say anything. If they did say anything, she would have been quick to say, "I'm ok."

"Mom, mom, said Carl. Stella turned white, and she collapsed on the floor. "Nicole, get me a face cloth, please! asked Carl. Nicole made the children sit on the sofa, and she got a wash cloth, rinsed it in cool water and passed it to Carl.

As Carl wiped his mom's forehead and cheeks, she started to groan. He retrieved a pillow and blanket from the bedroom, and he made her as comfortable as he could. When he mentioned the word "hospital" to Nicole, Stella started to make a fuss.

"No. no hospital." she cried.

"Mom, you are going to the hospital now, like it or not!" said Carl.

Carl went out the door to bring the car, as close to the house as possible. Before he helped his mom out to the car, he asked Nicole to call his brothers.

When Peter and Neils got to the hospital, Stella was hooked up to an IV, and a nurse was checking her blood pressure and pulse.

Everyone, but Stella remained quiet, while the nurse checked her vitals.

"Ok, can I go home now?" Stella asked.

"We'll see shortly. The doctor needs to see you first." said the nurse; He should be in a few minutes."

After the doctor came, everyone had to leave, while he made his assessment.

Peter and Neils asked Carl so many questions and, he got a little irritated. "Hey, Nicole and I just got home before Mom passed out; It's a good thing that we got home when we did!"

When the doctor came out of Stella's room, he looked at the three men, and called them aside.

"I'm keeping your mom in for a few days; I don't think it's serious, but she needs some rest, and a further examination."

"Thanks doctor, can we go back and visit with mom before we leave?" asked Carl.

"Sure, briefly; She is experiencing a concussion however, due to her fall." added the doctor.

When Carl got back from the hospital, Nicole was sitting with the kids, and she looked up and asked about Stella; She was so afraid when Stella collapsed.

"Mom's gonna be ok, the doctor is keeping her in for a few days." said Carl.

"I made us some supper, and I fed the kids, they were so hungry." said Nicole.

"I'm not hungry, right now." said Carl.

Nicole walked over to Carl and gave him a hug; "We can have something to eat after we put the kids to bed."

Soon, the children got their dad's attention, and together they played and giggled; Then, Carl and Nicole told a story to the children before they tucked them into bed.

Aaron's graduation was taking place in a couple of days; Everyone was excited, and busy with preparations. Stella was still in the hospital, and she wasn't very happy. "Carl, I must come home, she said, when he visited her. I can't miss Aaron's graduation!"

"Mom, we will take lots of pictures." said Carl

"But Carl she said, that's not the same."

"I know, added Carl. Peter will bring Aaron to visit you, dressed in his cap and gown. How will that be? "We can take pictures of you and him together."

"OK then, said Stella. I have a card with some money for Aaron on my dresser; Will you bring it to me so I can give it to Aaron myself?"

"Sure can, mom." replied Carl.

After the graduation, Nicole and Carl gave Stella's house a thorough cleaning, and a lot of repairs to the house and the shed. They wanted her house put in order before they left for Toronto. Stella wasn't returning home right away, however. She was going to stay at Neils briefly, until she got well enough to go home.

Chapter Twenty-Six

"Mom, I'm not listening!" said Marianne as she cupped her hands over her ears. Nicole and Marianne were forever arguing over one thing or another.

"I'm telling you Marianne, if you walk out that door right now, you're not coming back tonight!" said Nicole angrily.

"But mom, you don't understand!" added Marianne, just as she walked out the door, slamming it shut.

Marianne and Nicole had been butting heads over a boyfriend. The guy didn't measure up to Nicole's standards and Marianne told her mother, "Mom, I have graduated from high school, and I can make my own decisions!"

Marianne had some suitcases packed; They were in the trunk of her car just in case she decided to leave home. This time, it was her last straw with her mother, and she was leaving home and going to her grandmother Stella, to stay indefinitely.

"Where is Nicole?" asked Sam; He had just gotten home from school, and he needed to talk to her.

"She took off with her car, Sam." Nicole replied.

"Where did she go?" questioned Sam.

"Hard to say." replied Nicole. She didn't tell Sam that she and Marianne had another no-win argument. Sam resorted to his room; He would stay there until his dad came home for supper.

"Nicole, do you know where Marianne is, her car is gone?" questioned Carl, after he got home from work.

"No, I don't." replied Nicole. She wasn't telling Carl that she and Marianne had another big argument. "How was your day?" asked Nicole; She was trying to change the subject.

"Same as usual, replied Carl; Do you know where Marianne is?"

"No, I don't, she was so mad at me, she screamed and, took off with her car." Nicole replied.

"I wish you two could get along better." remarked Carl. He picked up the newspaper and resorted to the living room to relax.

When Marianne didn't return by ten o'clock, everyone was concerned, and worried. She didn't usually stay out late during the week.

Marianne knew that her family must be worried sick about her, so she called at six am. the next morning. By then, she would be closer to New Denmark and, nobody would stop her from going any further.

"Hello." said Carl when he picked up the phone. He was still groggy, and his voice revealed how he felt.

"Dad," Marianne started to say, but Carl was quicker to ask, "Where are you?"

"I'm at a service station." she replied.

"And, where are you going?" asked Carl.

"Grammy Stella's place." replied Marianne; Her lips were quivering, and Carl could tell that she was crying.

"That's ok, sweetie, I'll call gram and tell her that you are on your way; If you need anything, just call and let me know."

Marianne was quiet, she was still crying. "OK daddy."

"I love you sweetie." said Carl before he hung up.

"That had to be Marianne, said Nicole; Where is she?"

"At some service station; Were you too fighting again?" replied Carl.

Nicole's face took on a twisted look; She did not know what Carl was going to say next. Carl was so angry with Nicole, and he was at his wits end. He certainly wasn't empathizing with her now. He was calling his mom to let her know that Marianne was on her way to New Denmark.

Chapter Twenty-Seven

"Hey Carl, what's up said a co-worker; You're hammering those nails like a jack hammer!"

"Well, that's how I feel right now." replied Carl.

Carl wasn't going to talk about family issues at work, but he couldn't get his mind of what was happening at home.

Nicole, too, was having a bad day at work, and her staff could tell but, they did not discuss family issues at work either.

Both Nicole and Carl dreaded going home; They knew that a big argument was going to ensue.

"Nicole, I don't know what to say, said Carl; You pushed Marianne too far this time!"

Nicole didn't respond to Carl's statement, and she walked off to the washroom. Carl went to their bedroom, retrieved a suitcase and packed some clothes; He was leaving.

Sam walked up to his dad, when he saw the suitcase; "What's up with the suitcase, dad?"

"I'm going to the hotel for the night." replied Carl, and he continued his way out the door.

When Nicole came out of the washroom, Sam walked up to her and he asked, "Why is dad going to the hotel?"

"Aah, he must be really mad at me; He didn't tell me that he was leaving." said Nicole.

"And, did you find Marianne?" asked Sam.

"Yes, she went to New Denmark." said Nicole.

"What's for supper?" questioned Sam?"

"Whatever you can find; Help yourself." answered Nicole.

Carl knew that it was senseless to argue with Nicole; He called her after he arrived at the hotel and checked in.

Nicole raced to the phone; It had to be Carl. "Hello, Carl, thanks for telling me that you were leaving." said Nicole angrily.

"I didn't want to argue with you; I might have said something, really mean. I don't want regrets." said Carl.

"Eww, you make me so mad!" yelled Nicole, and she hung up.

Nicole called her dad and Marguerite. They empathized with her, somewhat; Though, they knew that both she and Carl possessed a strong will and either would give in to an argument.

Chapter Twenty-Eight

When Marianne arrived at her grandmother's place and knocked on her door, Stella was waiting, eagerly. She gave Marianne the biggest hug, "Come in, come in; I'm so happy to see you!" said Stella.

Marianne set her suitcase on the floor in the entry way, and she started to explain why she had come. "I know dad called you; Can I stay with you for awhile, please Gram?"

"Sure, said Stella, as long as you want." Then, Stella gave Marianne another hug. "Here, have a seat, Marianne; I'm getting a coffee and a lunch for us; Then, we can talk."

Marianne twisted and turned all night, and she heard her grandmother get up during the night several times.

When Marianne smelled coffee at daybreak, she knew her grandmother must be up for the day. That would be her cue to get dressed, and head out to the kitchen.

"Good morning, Marianne, breakfast is ready. I made some oatmeal, and there is plenty of fruit on the counter; Help yourself." said Stella as she poured herself a coffee. Stella wanted Marianne to make herself at home; That was why she said, "Help yourself."

Marianne never ate oatmeal in the morning, but she was polite, and she helped herself to a bowl.

"So, Gram, what are your plans for today?" asked Marianne.

"Nothing special, but since you are here, can you help me outside?" asked Stella.

Marianne and Stella weeded and rearranged the flower gardens. By the time they were finished, it was nearly lunch. "Gram, it's almost lunch time, would you go with me to Grand Falls; We can go to the diner at the Five 'n Ten for lunch."

"Oh Marianne, are you sure; We can make ourselves our own lunch." replied Stella.

"Yeah, Gram, we could, but I really would like to go to that diner." expressed Marianne.

"Well let's get cleaned up, and we'll go." said Stella.

The Five 'n Ten was the most popular store. It was more than a diner; It was a department store filled with everything from clothes to shoes and dishes. You name it, and you can buy it there, cheap. Usually, when Marianne and her family visited in New Denmark, they almost, always made a trip to the Five 'n Ten.

"Good day, Mrs. Larsen, Is this your grand daughter?" said the waitress as she passed them a menu.

"Yes, this is my granddaughter, Marianne." replied Stella.

"We have soup and sandwich on special, today." said the waitress, smiling.

When she returned to take their order, Stella said, "I'm having a chicken sandwich with coffee; What about you Marianne?"

"I'm having some French fries and a coke." answered Marianne.

"That's all you are going to eat?" asked Stella.

"Well, I'm having dessert after, a piece of Lemon Meringue Pie." added Marianne.

"Sounds good, I'll have one too." added Stella.

After they ate, they shopped until three pm.; They were going home to pick some rhubarb and then, make some supper. "Do you still like Danish Sausages, Marianne?"

"Sure do, with applesauce and baked potatoes."

"So, let's get busy, and we can make some rhubarb crumble for dessert." said Stella.

"I have never eaten rhubarb crumble; Mom never has rhubarb." said Marianne.

"Ohh, it's so good, you can help me make it." said Stella.

After supper, Stella and Marianne cleaned up the dishes. Stella was going to watch the news, and Marianne was calling home.

Chapter Twenty-Nine

"Hello." said Sam when he answered the phone; Marianne was calling.

"Where's mom or dad?" she asked.

"They went somewhere for the weekend." replied Sam.

"And they left you all alone, surprising." said Marianne.

"You don't have to say it like that!" expressed Sam with a disgruntled voice.

"I'll call back later." said Marianne, and she hung up before Sam could say more.

Carl and Nicole were due for a weekend by themselves, so they drove to Niagara Falls, and booked into a hotel.

At the Skylon Tower, they ate in the dining room, and then they climbed the stairs to the observation deck, the best view of the falls. Then, they shopped the gift shops, buying special gifts for everyone. Niagara Falls was a truly wonderful escape from the everyday grind of work and home.

"You know Carl, we should do this more often." said Nicole.

"Yeah, I agree, said Carl; Let's go back to our room."

They stayed at Niagara Falls until ten o'clock that evening. It was an hour drive home, and they were not rushing things.

"Mom, dad, is that you?" called Sam from the living room. He had fallen asleep on the sofa, waiting for his parents. He missed them, and he wanted to catch up with the latest happenings.

"Not tonight Sam, said Carl; Your mom and I are tired. Could we catch up tomorrow night?"

"Sure, Sam replied, Goodnight Mom, Good night Dad."

Chapter Thirty

"Do you think we should plan a vacation?" said Nicole, one night after their weekend in Niagara Falls.

"Sure do, how about going back to Niagara Falls?" asked Carl.

"You're kidding!" remarked Nicole.

"Yes, I'm kidding, let's check our savings, and we'll take three weeks." suggested Carl.

"Why three weeks?" asked Nicole.

"Well, if we take our vacation on Thanks-Giving weekend, we'll actually have enough time for one month, right." said Carl.

"Right!" Nicole replied, and she hit him with a pillow from their bed.

Carl knocked Nicole down on their bed, and he started to tickle her; Then he kissed her so passionately.

"Think about this Nicole, said Carl, my Aunt Elizabeth lives in Southern California and."

Nicole finished for Carl, "And, we can spend our vacation with her!"

"Yes, what do you think?" asked Carl, searching Nicole's face, which had a puzzled look.

"And what's so great about California?" she asked.

"Southern California, Southern California dear." repeated Carl. "Listen to me, I'll explain about the place." added Carl.

"Reason one, Aunt Elizabeth lives alone on a great big ranch; Reason two, she is wealthy, reason three, we'll get a super tan, while we go hiking and horseback riding." suggested Carl.

"Have you ever gone horse back riding?" interrupted Nicole.

"No, we can have fun learning!" stated Carl.

"We, you said we!" I am not getting on a horse, Carl." exclaimed Nicole.

"And, we can stay in her bunk house." said Carl.

"I'm liking the idea, better! exclaimed Nicole, when do we leave?"

Elizabeth, Carls' aunt lived on a huge ranch in Southern California. In her younger days, she had a rich pen pal, James Carsten. James invited Elizabeth to come for a visit; They fell in love, and Elizabeth stayed in Southern California.

James' siblings were always trying to run his life, especially after their parents were killed in a tragic accident. James became sole owner of the ranch, and his brother and sister were entrusted with a huge amount of money.

Elizabeth and James got married by the local pastor, right on the ranch. They had a small private wedding, with best friends only.

The ranch kept them busy; James appointed Elizabeth as Accountant, cook and a helper, whenever and wherever she was needed. James was the charge person; He looked after the hired hands, making sure everything and everybody was looked after.

Eight years later, James developed major health issues, and even with the best of care, he passed away quietly.

Because James and Elizabeth had no children, Elizabeth became sole owner of the ranch.

Chapter Thirty-One

"So, Nicole, what do you think about spending a month with Aunt Elizabeth?" asked Carl.

"I think we should call your aunt and start making plans." replied Nicole.

Elizabeth was delighted to have Carl and Nicole visit, and she was looking forward to having some family around.

When Carl and Nicole arrived at the airport, Elizabeth was waiting for them with much anticipation. It was not difficult to spot Elizabeth in the crowd, with her white cowboy hat, plaid shirt, jeans and cowboy boots. She dressed like a rancher; She even drove a red convertible with steer horns decorating the hood. Carl expected his aunt to be speaking with a southern accent, however, she spoke simple English with a hint of a Danish accent.

"Carl, Nicole, I am so happy to have you visit with me she said, giving them each a quick hug. Sometimes, since James passed away, I've gotten so very lonely. If you do not mind, I plan on having you stay at the main house with me."

"Sure, we understand." said Carl and Nicole in unison. Nicole and Carl were in awe, when they came in sight of the ranch house and its spectacular surroundings, the buildings, flower gardens and the trees. It was kinda' like in the movies, but it was better because it was real.

"Hello, Mr. and Mrs. Larsen, I'm Lance, one of the work hands. Let me help you with your bags."

"Thanks Lance." said Carl as he shook the mans' hand. Nicole was still admiring the place.

Elizabeth took Carl and Nicole to their room, explained that fresh coffee and tea was available with some snacks, anytime. They could freshen up and perhaps rest for awhile. She would be somewhere in the house if they needed her.

Nicole and Carl looked at each other, then they both fell on the double size bed. Nicole got up and rested on her elbow. "You know Carl, I've never seen such a beautiful, but practical place, in all my years in real-estate."

"I could adapt to this place quite easily!" expressed Carl.

After they both rested, they showered and dressed. Then they sauntered into the private dining room for coffee, crackers and cheese. Elizabeth was in the big kitchen preparing supper, so Carl and Nicole ventured outside. The back yard was breath-taking with the trees, shrubs, and flowers. A large pool was near the tiled deck, and water fountains cascaded over rocks making rippling sounds. There were some orchards nearby, and a huge vegetable garden. A dirt road led to the horse stable, and the chicken coup, and on endlessly to grasslands.

"I'm glad you suggested coming here for vacation, Carl." said Nicole.

"Me, too; it's more beautiful than I imagined." said Carl.

They sat outside until Elizabeth came out to say, "We will have supper at seven, after the hired hands finish eating their supper."

"Would you like some help, we'd love to help." said Nicole.

"Sure, that would be great!" replied Elizabeth.

"Show us the way." said Carl

The men had just started a queue to get their plates. All drinks and utensils were on the table. When everyone was seated, one of the guys gave thanks.

A conversation flowed among the men regarding their daily happenings. Everyone was polite and welcoming, and instead of waiting for supper at seven, tonight Elizabeth, Nicole and Carl joined the men for supper. After dessert was served, each worker resorted to their private bunk houses.

Carl and Nicole helped Elizabeth clean up the dining room, and dishes. "Whew, said Elizabeth, wiping her brow, it always feels like a storm just passed through!"

"Perhaps you should hire some help in the kitchen, Aunt Elizabeth." said Carl.

"You are right Carl, I'm not so young anymore! said Elizabeth. Let's go sit out back for awhile and chat."

"Aunt Liz, can I call you that, said Nicole; How do you manage everything?"

"Well, I'm used to this, and the hired hands assume a lot of responsibility. These five guys have worked on this ranch for many years. Some worked for James' parents, when they operated the ranch."

"So, what happens to this place when you retire?" asked Carl.

"Well, I do have a will, but it's one day at a time; I am so happy here." replied Elizabeth.

"So, it's your vacation, you're free to explore the ranch, go shopping, relax, whatever?" suggested Elizabeth. "By the way, would you like to have a ride in my old Chevy? I want to show you this four-hundred-acre ranch of mine, she said; Carl, you can drive."

As Carl drove slowly over a dirt road, Elizabeth pointed out places of interest. "That place over there, on the other side of that stone wall, I have a sheep farm. And, over there is my escape from everything, ten acres of hardwood surrounding a freshwater lake."

"Oh, look at those horses, Carl." exclaimed Nicole.

"Those are wild horses, they like the fields and the woods, here." said Elizabeth.

"Well, we must get back, and I'll show you around the house and yard some more another time, said Elizabeth; Drop Nicole and I off near the walk, Carl and then, put the pick-up in the garage, please."

Nicole and Carl did take Elizabeth's suggestions about enjoying hikes, and picnics. Sometimes they relaxed by themselves, and sometimes with Elizabeth, reminiscing about old times. There was no end to stories told and untold.

Chapter Thirty-Two

"Just watch me!" said Carl; He was showing off as he was mounting a horse saddled and waiting. After a few lessons, he had the mount conquered, and he could ride the horse along the dirt road quite well. Nicole watched only because she was afraid to try. Carl did this each evening after supper, when a ranch hand was able to ride with him.

Eventually, Carl and Nicole doubled up on the horse, and headed to the woods for a picnic. They fished at the lake, and they usually caught enough fish for lunch.

One day, while riding near a brook, something startled the horse, and both Carl and Nicole fell off. "Are you OK, Nicole?" asked Carl.

"Yeah, I think so, Nicole replied, What about you?"

"I'm not sure, I can't sit up, and my shoulder hurts, so bad." said Carl moaning in pain.

"God, please help." prayed Nicole. Her only option to help Carl was to get on the horse and go for help.

"Tell me what to do, please Carl."

Despite the pain, Carl told Nicole what to do, and shortly after, she was in the saddle leaving for the ranch.

Elizabeth saw Nicole coming up the dusty road toward the house, alone. She hurried from the front porch to meet her. "Nicole, where's Carl?"

"He's hurt; Can you go with me, Aunt Liz?" cried Nicole.

"Yeah, said Elizabeth, you can drive the pickup, and I'll take the horse and follow you."

Together, they reached Carl, who was still lying near the stream.

"Here, Carl, hug Nicole with your right arm, and I'll brace your back; We can do this!" instructed Elizabeth.

Carl moaned and soon, he was on his feet, still moaning.

"Let's get you to the truck, and to the hospital." said Elizabeth.

Nicole was frightened and she wasn't saying much until they were on their way to the hospital.

"Great, that's just great, I'm so sorry Nicole, expressed Carl; This is our vacation."

"Don't worry Carl, our vacation is not over yet; We just won't go horseback riding any more." replied Nicole.

Soon they arrived at the hospital emergency; Someone took Carl by stretcher to the emergency room. The doctor checked him over and, had him X rayed. He had a broken collarbone and a few bumps.

"You will see a lot of discoloration tomorrow, and you'll experience a lot of pain." said the doctor; A nurse gave Carl a shot for the pain and the doctor handed him a prescription for some pain medication.

Elizabeth called the hospital when she got back to the ranch; She was relieved to hear that Carl was coming home.

Chapter Thirty-Three

Nicole and Carl had a few days left before they left for Toronto, and it was a pleasure assisting Elizabeth in any way they could until that day.

And sadly, the day arrived when Elizabeth drove them to the airport with her red convertible. She sat with them until the announcement came to board the plane; Then, they hugged and hugged again. Elizabeth watched until Nicole and Carl were boarded, and the plane was out of sight. Tears were flooding her eyes, not only with sadness, but with a renewed hope to see them again.

"Mom, Dad!" exclaimed Sam and Marianne together, when their parents approached them near the entrance to the airport. Nicole and Carl were surprised to see Marianne and Sam together; They hugged and shed a few tears of joy.

Everyone started to talk at the same time, until Carl said "Whoa; Let's take turns, ok; Let's get these suitcases into the car, and then go home."

"We will have to call Dad and Marguerite and invite them over." said Nicole.

"For sure!" added Carl.

"Can we get takeout for supper first? Marianne asked, I am hungry."

"Me too, said Sam; I'll call in our order when we get home."

Nicole called her dad and Marguerite right after she got in the door; "Hi Dad, we just got home; Do you and Marguerite want to come over, for a while?"

"We sure do, we'll be there in a few minutes." replied Sam.

Just then, a knock came to the door; It was the delivery man. Nicole paid him, took the food and carried their meal to the kitchen, and informed everyone that supper was ready. Before everyone got to sit at the table, there were more knocks at the door.

"It must be dad and Marguerite; I'll check." said Nicole.

"Dad, Marguerite, you didn't take long; Were you speeding?" asked Nicole.

"A little bit." remarked Sam.

"Lucky, there were no police cars on the road." said Marguerite.

"Come in and have supper with us." called out Carl from the kitchen.

When Sam saw Carls' arm in a sling, he asked. "What happened to you, Carl? Did Nicole twist your arm?"

"Not this time; I fell off a horse." replied Carl

"Well that explains it; What else have you two been doing?" asked Sam. Marguerite remained quiet, she was listening, however.

"Dad, we helped Elizabeth on the ranch, like mucking horse stalls. We helped prepare some meals for the ranch hands, and we ate with them."

"But you were on vacation!" interrupted Sam.

"We know." replied Carl as he watched Nicole's face; She was lit up like a Christmas tree.

"See my tan, said Nicole; It was so warm every day, and we spent most of our time outside."

Nicole and Carl had so many stories to tell, and it was getting late. Sam looked at the clock and exclaimed, "Nine o'clock, we gotta go!"

"We are tired, said Nicole; Can we get together for supper again tomorrow night?"

"It's a plan." said Sam as he walked to the door with Marguerite.

"Whew, I'm bushed! said Carl; I'm going to bed."

"I'm right behind you!" exclaimed Nicole.

Chapter Thirty-Four

Soon everything was back to normal. Nicole and Marianne picked up from the past and fought daily. Perhaps, that is what happens when girls grow up, and still live at home. No house they say, is big enough for more than one woman.

"Marianne where is our supper?" asked Nicole.

"Still in the fridge." responded Marianne.

"Still in the fridge!" reiterated Nicole; "Well, you can start making supper, right now!"

Marianne grumbled, as she searched for something to prepare.

Nicole waited for Carl to get home; "I don't know what to do, she said. I asked Marianne to make our supper, and she didn't."

"Did you ask her why?" replied Carl?

"No, and now she won't speak to me." said Nicole.

"I don't know about you two, we gotta do something; You can't be fighting all the time." said Carl.

"I know, said Nicole, got any answers?"

"Let's have supper; Then, we'll see if we can find some answers." replied Carl.

Within an hour, supper was ready, and everyone was sitting at the table sharing events of the day.

"Dad, Aunt Elizabeth called, said Marianne; She wants you to call her back."

"Thanks, Marianne, I'll do that; I wonder what she wants." said Carl swallowing a bite of his supper.

"Marianne, would you like to visit with your aunt for awhile?" asked Carl.

"Yeah, I love too, when can I go?" asked Marianne.

"We'll see, said Carl; I'll ask her, when I call her later."

"Lucky you." suggested Sam.

"No one said that Marianne is going anywhere! said Nicole, as she started to clear the table. Come on, Marianne, you're doing the dishes."

Nicole and Carl went to their bedroom after supper to make a phone call to Elizabeth in private.

"Aunt Elizabeth, said Carl; Marianne said you called."

"Yeah, I realized I needed some help in the kitchen, do you think I could hire Marianne?"

"That would be great, we'll ask her, just hold on a second." said Carl.

"No, no, Carl, ask Marianne first, and she can call me back, said Elizabeth. How are you and Nicole doing? Is your shoulder healing ok; I still feel so bad about that!"

"Don't worry about that, I'm ok; Can't wait to get on a horse again, remarked Carl; Nicole wants to say hi, I'll chat later," he said as he passed the phone to Nicole.

"I'm fine, Aunt Elizabeth, Nicole replied; I am back to work."

After the phone conversation with Elizabeth, Nicole and Carl looked at each other, smiled, and hugged. Perhaps, the issue about Marianne and Nicole's arguments was resolved.

Chapter Thirty-Five

"Aunt Elizabeth needs a helper, Marianne; Would you like to work for her?" asked Nicole.

"Oh, that would be a dream come true; When do I start?" asked Marianne.

"Slow down, Marianne, said Nicole, it will be hard work, and a commitment that must not be broken when things get tough!"

"When can I start?" questioned Marianne.

"As soon as you can get packed, and when we get you there said Carl; I'll call Aunt Elizabeth right now."

At five o'clock the next day, Marianne was meeting her great aunt at the airport. When Marianne saw the red convertible, she was ecstatic.

"This is what you drive Auntie Liz!" said Marianne as she loaded her suitcases into the car.

"Only when I travel for social events; I drive a pick-up for ranch work." Elizabeth replied.

"I'm so excited to see the ranch, Auntie; Can I call you Auntie?" asked Marianne.

"Call me anything, but late for supper." replied Elizabeth.

"How long will it take to get to the ranch?" asked Marianne.

"Less than an hour, are you hungry?" questioned Elizabeth.

"Yeah, Auntie," replied Marianne.

"There is a roadside restaurant nearby; We'll stop there first." said Elizabeth.

Marianne was impressed with the menu, and she had a difficult time choosing something.

"Try the Angus cheeseburger and fries, one of my favorites." said Elizabeth.

"With a coke......," said Marianne.

After they finished their meal, Elizabeth took the tab, and she tipped the waiter.

"Ok, ready to go, Marianne; We'll be at the ranch in fifteen minutes." said Elizabeth.

Marianne's mouth flew open; She was in awe as she took in the sight of the ranch. She had only seen places like this on television.

"What do you think, Marianne?" asked Elizabeth, as she pulled up in the driveway.

"I'm speechless!" replied Marianne.

When the car came to a stop, this young handsome man walked to Elizabeth's door. "Hello mam, let me help you and the young lady." he said tipping his cowboy hat.

"Sure, get this young lady's suitcases from the back." replied Elizabeth.

"I'm pleased to meet you miss……said the man as he reached to shake Marianne's hand; Let me help you with your bags." he said staring at her.

After walking to the front porch, Marianne stood momentarily, taking in the view.

"I'll show you around Marianne, after I catch my breath; I'm not so young anymore. Have a seat over here, and we'll have a little chat, ok." said Elizabeth.

"Well, let us see where I start; First, the young man you met is Jacob Frieze, my foreman. I couldn't manage this place without him. You can count on him too, for help around this place." explained Elizabeth. Your responsibility will be helping me mostly around the kitchen, cooking, cleaning and running errands. What do you think?"

"When do I start?" asked Marianne.

"Right away, said Elizabeth, after I show you around."

Chapter Thirty-Six

Elizabeth drew up a general guide for the day, just in case she would forget something. Since Marianne was starting, Elizabeth posted the daily guide on a bulletin board. "Marianne, she said, I have set up a bulletin board to post menus etc. I will still share my plans with you, as we will be working side by side most of the time."

The first thing on the agenda is breakfast; "You can start with the coffee, Marianne. The instructions are posted on the coffee percolator; I will get the bacon and sausages." continued Elizabeth.

The night before, Elizabeth had set the big table in the dining room with jams, sugar, salt and pepper and all the dishes, utensils and napkins. Then, she placed a huge bowl of fresh fruit on a small table near the entry way.

When the men came in before breakfast, they hung their hats and jackets in the hallway. Then, they proceeded to the table to pick up their plates and follow each other in queue. Everything was served buffet style, except for the coffee. Generally, Elizabeth poured the hot coffee or tea, but now, it was Marianne's job. The men started to talk all at once, until Elizabeth interrupted them. "Hey guys, slow down; This is my assistant, Marianne. She came all the way from Toronto, Canada to work with me! Please be polite and welcome her."

Marianne blushed and said, "Hi."

Soon the men were discussing their daily chores and plans, while finishing their breakfast. Then, they donned their cowboy hats, and followed Jacob to the workshop. Jacob gave the men their daily work order and allowed them time to discuss whatever.

Elizabeth and Marianne helped themselves to breakfast and coffee, before they cleaned up the dishes and the dining hall. The next thing on the agenda was routine housekeeping, baking, and preparing supper.

"Marianne, Jacob is going to town, would you go with him and pick up a few things on this list? asked Elizabeth. That will be a good chance for you to become familiar with everyone and everything around here."

"OK, when do I go?" asked Marianne.

"Right now, Jacob is waiting outside in the truck." added Elizabeth.

"Ok, Auntie."

"Now, get going."

Jacob and Marianne made eye contact when she got into the pickup, then they both turned their heads.

"Well Marianne, what do you think about the ranch?" asked Jacob.

"It's beautiful, and there's so much to take in." replied Marianne.

"It won't take long to adapt, I know!" responded Jacob.

For the rest of the trip, Marianne and Jacob became quiet and, they focused on their reasons to go into town.

The first place they stopped, was at the local market with a huge grocery store nearby. There were shops and homes lining the street ahead of them. They would check them out later.

"I'll drop you off here, and I'll go to the hardware. Then, I will pick you up in forty-five minutes, ok." suggested Jacob.

Marianne grabbed her basket, as she got out of the pickup and headed toward the market, without saying anything. She took her list from her shirt pocket, as she checked out the fruit and vegetables. Then, she went into the grocery store. Her mouth opened with awe as she gazed at the displays. This store wasn't like the grocery store in Toronto. It was huge; Everything was grouped, and a staff worker was available in each department. After she picked up what she needed, she headed back to the door, where there were several cash registers with attendants.

She had finished her shopping before Jacob got back, so she waited briefly. Jacob pulled the pickup up into the parking lot, got out and sauntered over to help her.

"Next stop, Maggie's diner for lunch; Are you hungry?" he asked.

"A bit." replied Marianne with a shy look on her face. She didn't have much pocket money, and she was relieved to know that the meal was covered by Elizabeth's expense account.

Upon entering the diner, Marianne noticed the décor, totally Western style with Country western music blaring from a jukebox. The place was bustling with people, and it was noisy.

"There's a booth right over there." said Jacob, pointing to the place. They barely got seated before a waitress came to take their order. While they ate, Jacob told Marianne about the different places she might like to check out sometime.

The ride home was relatively quiet, except when Jacob shared bits about life at the ranch.

"How was your first trip into town, Marianne?" asked Elizabeth, after Marianne and Jacob carried in the groceries.

"Interesting Auntie." replied Marianne. "Thanks for lunch, the cheeseburger and fries were the best!" she exclaimed.

"You're welcome," Now, let's get supper, baked potatoes and Spaghetti, and apple crisp for dessert." said Elizabeth.

CHAPTER THIRTY-SEVEN

Jacob let out a loud whistle when he saw Marianne out in the vegetable garden. Her hair was flowing loosely in the slight breeze, as she bent over gathering some string beans for supper. She was wearing a red plaid shirt over a black camisole and capris. She looked up, smiled and gave him a quick wave.

Jacob walked over to her; "Need some help?" he asked.

"Yeah, no I'm kidding; What are you up too?" she asked.

"I was wondering if we could go horseback riding on Saturday?" he asked, bending over to pick a few beans.

Marianne didn't want to sound desperate about becoming better acquainted with Jacob, so she hesitated to give him an answer. She told him that she'd ask her aunt first.

Of course, Elizabeth smiled and said, "Sure, anytime after seven o'clock."

Marianne had never gone horseback riding, ever before. She dressed in a plaid flannel shirt over a camisole top and blue jean. She wore running shoes since she didn't own a pair of cowboy boots, yet; Then, she wore her ball cap, since she didn't have a cowboy hat, yet.

Jacob gave his famous whistle when he rode up to the front porch on his horse, Gallop.

"All ready, Marianne?"

"You'll have to help me, Jacob; I've never rode horseback before." she told him.

"Ok, I'll help you." he said as he instructed her, until she was seated in front of him on Gallop. They started slowly and, picked up the pace gradually. As they toured the trails, Marianne became absorbed with her surroundings, and of course, listening to Jacobs' stories about the life of a rancher.

"Look, Jacob, exclaimed Marianne when she saw wild horses grazing beside a lake; Are they Aunties?" she asked.

"No, they're wild horses, they come here often." explained Jacob.

"Wow!" exclaimed Marianne, as she admired the horses and their exquisite beauty.

It was getting dusk, and Jacob was heading back to the house. "What do you think Marianne; Do you want to do this again?" he asked.

"For sure! exclaimed Marianne, I'll get some boots and a cowboy hat for our next ride."

Each passing day, Marianne was getting better acquainted with her aunt, her job, coworkers and the whole ranch in general, and she loved every bit of it. She called her parents occasionally, to catch up on the latest family news. She was somewhat lonesome, especially when she talked on the phone. "How's Grampie Sam and Marguerite?" she asked; How's Grammie Stella?" She always called her grammie Larsen, Grammie Stella; Sam took the phone.

Her brother Sam missed her a great deal. "Hi sis, how's it going?"

"Great Sam, I miss you, Sam; How's school?"

"Oh, the usual; I have a girlfriend Marianne, don't tell mom and dad, they don't know yet?"

"So, who is she, Sam?"

"Her father is the Baptist minister."

"Wow, you mean Sarah, sweet Sarah! exclaimed Marianne; Let me talk to dad, please."

"Dad, do you think you could sell my car; I don't need it, and I could use the money, right now," asked Marianne.

"I'll see what I can do, Marianne; I love you, sweetie; Your mom wants to say something."

"Marianne, don't be afraid to ask us for anything; You know we love you!"

Marianne did not add any remarks to her mother's statement, told her that she loved her, and said good-bye.

Chapter Thirty-Eight

"Marianne, can you take care of breakfast?" asked Elizabeth. "Sure Auntie, got it!" replied Marianne as she started a pot of coffee. Elizabeth was not feeling so good this morning; She was going to relax for the day.

When Jacob and the ranch hands came in for breakfast, and they didn't see Elizabeth, they started to ask Marianne questions about her aunt. Marianne heard them exchanging their concerns regarding Elizabeth. Jacob spoke up on their behalf, "Marianne, please let us know how Elizabeth is doing?"

"For sure, Jacob, I'm checking in on her after I clean things up; I'll walk over to your place, and let you know."

"Thanks Marianne." he said tipping his hat to her.

Elizabeth was restless in her bed; She had a bad headache, and she felt weak. "Auntie, I'm getting Jacob, and we're taking you to the hospital, right now." she said.

Elizabeth made no fuss, and soon they were at the hospital. Elizabeth's family doctor was on call, and he made a quick assessment of Elizabeth's condition. Jacob was listed as next of kin, so the doctor called him in to his office.

"Jacob, Elizabeth has taken a small stroke; I'm admitting her now, so I can make a further assessment. She'll need a lot of rest. She told me about Marianne, her niece, working for her. Thank goodness, because she is slowing down."

Marianne stayed by her auntie, who was resting on a stretcher in the emergency ward. Both Elizabeth and Marianne were afraid, and anxious to hear what the doctor had to say.

"Auntie said Marianne, when the nurse came to help Elizabeth into bed. I am going with Jacob to pack you some clothes, and then, we'll be back after supper, OK?"

"OK, Marianne, and thank you sweetie." said Elizabeth. Marianne and Elizabeth hugged, and held on to each other, while Jacob waited for his turn.

Jacob gave Elizabeth a soft kiss on her forehead, after he took off his cowboy hat. Then he put the hat on again and tipped it to her. "Don't worry, I got this, take care, mam!" Then he left, before he could see Elizabeth's tears.

Both Marianne and Jacob were quiet on the way home, as they were thinking about so many changes that were about to happen.

That night Marianne called home. "Oh, mom, said Marianne as she cried to her. "Auntie is in the hospital; she took a stroke!"

"Ohhh Marianne, I'm so sorry, your dad is in the living room, just a minute; Carl, pickup the phone."

"Daddy, Auntie took a stroke." she said, sobbing and wiping her eyes and nose with her hands, and forearm.

"Marianne, be strong and take charge for Auntie, ok; You can do it!" he said.

"Yeah dad, she replied, wiping away the tears streaming down her face; I can do it!"

Marianne and her parents discussed details about Elizabeth's situation and plans for her future on the ranch. They caught up on the latest news at home and, Sam came on the line to say hello.

Marianne felt much better after talking with her family, and she was assured that she could take charge with her responsibilities.

Chapter Thirty-Nine

After a week in the hospital, Elizabeth came home. She was impressed with Marianne's housekeeping; Everything was immaculate. "I'm so proud of you, Marianne; You are amazing, sweetie."

Marianne and Jacob were doting on Elizabeth, until she stopped them in their tracks, "Stop fussing over me, and get back to work. We must get supper! Marianne, you can prepare the vegetables."

Marianne tried to tell Elizabeth that supper was prepared, already; But, she had to let Elizabeth find out for herself.

This evening, Marianne and Elizabeth joined the ranch hands for supper; The guys were all anxious about being updated by Elizabeth, personally, regarding her hospital stay.

After supper, Elizabeth let Marianne clean up; She was tired, and she needed a rest.

Elizabeth called Marianne into the living room later; "Marianne, would you get Jacob; You and I and Jacob need a little chat."

"Sure Auntie, I'll be right back." said Marianne.

"Mam, said Jacob when he faced Elizabeth, tipping his hat to her; You wanted to see me?"

"Yes, it's time for me to make some decisions, regarding the ranch; I want you and Marianne's input."

"Sit." said Elizabeth, as she waved to two empty chairs.

"Jacob, you've been with me for a few years; You're like family, so I'm willing a hundred grand to you; You may have to find a new home, down the road."

Jacob started to speak; However, Elizabeth would not let him. Then, she turned to Marianne. "Marianne, I'm giving this ranch to your dad!"

"And, continued Elizabeth, Marianne, I'm paying for your tuition for University or college, whatever you choose."

Marianne was about to say something, when Elizabeth put her pointer finger on her lower lip and went "schuh; She had the final say. I'm calling my lawyer tomorrow, to have everything down on paper."

Everyone remained quiet until Elizabeth asked Marianne to get them coffee and some cookies; Then, they sat in front of the fireplace, chatting and watching some television.

Chapter Forty

Jacob found Marianne in the garden, picking vegetables. When he spoke, he startled her. "Sorry, Marianne, just wanted to know if you'll go riding with me on Saturday."

"Yeah sure!" replied Marianne. "Would you give me a hand with these vegetables? We need them for supper."

"What's for supper?" asked Jacob, as he pulled out some nice carrots.

"Roast Beef with gravy and vegetables." replied Marianne.

"My favorite." remarked Jacob.

"And apple pie, that's why I want you to pick some of those apples." added Marianne as she pointed to the apple orchard.

Saturday evening, Jacob walked over to Elizabeth's place. Elizabeth was sitting on the front porch, hoping to have a quick chat with him.

"Jacob, I overheard Marianne sobbing, in her room last night. Do you have any idea why?"

"No mam." replied Jacob.

"You wouldn't be keeping anything from me, would you?" questioned Elizabeth as she stared him down.

"No mam." said Jacob; Just then, Marianne came bouncing out the door, all dressed for riding.

"Have fun, you two, and be careful!" said Elizabeth as Jacob and Marianne rode away on Gallop.

They rode to the beautiful valley, where the wild horses grazed, and drank their fill from the cool bubbling brook. The scenery was breathtaking with the skies filled with much color, after the setting sun.

"Let's sit here for a while, suggested Jacob; The horse needs to rest before we go home."

They found a windfallen tree to sit on; "It feels almost magical here, like nature speaking." whispered Marianne.

"I feel and hear the magic every time I come here." said Jacob as he wrapped his arms around Marianne and gazed towards the brook.

"Marianne, do you have dreams, I mean, hopes for your future?" asked Jacob?

Marianne's eyes filled with tears, and she stood before she told him about Chris, her fiancée.

"I'm sorry, Marianne; I didn't mean to pry." added Jacob.

"That's all right, Jacob; I needed to talk to someone about Chris. I really do."

Jacob got quiet, then Marianne started to tell Jacob her story.

"Mom and dad don't know about Chris; They expected me to go to college right after graduation. They wouldn't understand that I was in love. And Chris wouldn't meet their criteria."

"Well, are you and Chris keeping in touch; You've been here for quite some time?" asked Jacob.

"Yes, we've been writing letters, but Chris wants more than letters, right now." said Marianne.

Jacob remained quiet. "Chris wants me to quit my job here and go back to be with him." added Marianne.

"You know, Marianne, Elizabeth needs you more than ever." explained Jacob.

"I know, Jacob, but Chris is hurting, right now, added Marianne, and it's my fault."

"Don't blame yourself. When I asked you about your dreams, they are your hopes for your future. Jacob stopped talking momentarily, then he added, we'd better get back, it's getting late."

Chapter Forty-One

"Wake up Auntie, wake up Auntie." Marianne was hysterical when Elizabeth did not respond, and she ran to Jacob's cabin. "Jacob, Auntie won't wake up, hurry." she cried.

Jacob grabbed his t-shirt and ran bare feet to the ranch house; Marianne followed him.

Elizabeth was unresponsive, and her breathing was very weak. "Marianne, call 911 now." he demanded as he ran a hand through his hair, and he started to pace the floor.

The ambulance arrived within a half hour. The attendants got Elizabeth onto a stretcher quickly and, got her into the ambulance; They assessed her vitals on the way to the hospital. Marianne and Jacob followed behind.

When they brought Elizabeth into the hospital, the ambulance attendants looked at each other, and shook their heads; Elizabeth was gone. Marianne and Jacob entered in the emergency doors, and instantly they knew.

Marianne's hand flew to her mouth in shock; She looked toward Jacob, as he turned his back.

A nurse came to Marianne and Jacob, and she directed them to a private room. There, they were able to say their final goodbyes to Elizabeth and do whatever was deemed necessary at the time.

"Marianne, said Jacob, let's get back to the house; We got lots to take care off."

Well, the ranch hands had gotten their breakfast, and left for work. Marianne and Jacob got themselves some coffee and an apple fritter. They had no appetite, but they needed something to keep going. They discussed what they thought would soon take precedence at the ranch, and together they cleaned up the dishes and the dining room.

Jacob went to his bunkhouse, and Marianne called her parents. She dreaded making the phone call, but she did what she had to.

Marianne knew her parents would be at work, so she called her mom. "Hi mom. are you sitting down?"

"No, why Marianne, said Nicole as she walked to her office door and closed it. Marianne," she repeated.

"Mom, cried Marianne, Auntie."

"Marianne, what about Auntie?" asked Nicole.

Marianne was having trouble saying that her Auntie had just passed away; "Mom, please tell dad, I gotta go!" and she hung up.

Nicole tried calling Marianne back, but could not, because the phone had fallen off the receiver.

Marianne took a quick shower, got dressed and did the rest of the housework. She had to plan supper for the ranch hands.

Jacob came over before supper to help Marianne. "I tried to call you, but I kept getting a busy signal." he said.

"Oh no, she said as she put the phone back on the receiver; I wondered why the phone didn't ring."

"How did you make out calling your mom, Marianne?" asked Jacob.

"All right, I guess; I fell apart a bit, and I cried a bit; I have never experienced dying before." said Marianne. "Mom and dad are calling me back as soon as they know what their plans will be." added Marianne.

"Your Auntie had her will prepared, and it pretty well said what she wants. Thank God! expressed Jacob; I have made the necessary arrangements, also."

Marianne remained quiet briefly, until Jacob told her that he'd keep her up to date on the funeral arrangements.

"Thank you, Jacob, I appreciate all you've done." she said.

Jacob stepped closer to Marianne, and they hugged each other.

Chapter Forty-Two

Nicole, Carl and Sam arrived at the airport a day before the funeral; Marianne was relieved.

It was Sam's first visit to the ranch; Like his mom, dad and Marianne, he was in awe. Unfortunately, he'd never get to really know his great Aunt.

When everyone arrived at the ranch house, Jacob was waiting to greet them at the front door. He tipped his hat to welcome everybody, and introduced himself to Sam.

"Take time to find your rooms, and freshen up, he said; Marianne can assist you; Ok, Marianne."

"Ok, Jacob; Does anybody want a coffee or tea; Sam, a glass of milk or coke?" Marianne knew Sam didn't drink coffee or tea.

"Not right now, Marianne, we just want to find our rooms, and meet with Jacob later; What time is supper?" asked Nicole.

"Around six, we still have a couple of hours." explained Marianne.

"I'll help you with supper, Marianne; I used to help Auntie all the time." said Nicole.

"Mom, I'm glad you are here; I've been so sad and lonely since Auntie." Marianne couldn't say anymore, and Nicole wrapped her arms around her, and they cried together.

"Mmm, something smells good in here." said Jacob. He came into the kitchen early, just to see how everything was going."

Marianne looked up at Jacob, "Great!" she said.

"Where's Sam and Carl?" he asked.

"They're in the back." said Nicole; "Carl is showing Sam around."

"Well, I'm going to join them, ok." said Jacob looking at Marianne for approval of some sort.

Chapter Forty-Three

Elizabeth's funeral was held in the small Anglican church in town. The intermittent was at her graveside, next to her husband, James. They shared the same headstone, and their graves were on the same lot, not far from a small stream on the ranch. They would be forever home, together.

Jacob shared the eulogy at the graveside, because Elizabeth wanted that. She wanted James' siblings to know, just how much she loved her husband. She wanted them to know also, how much she loved and dedicated herself to the ranch.

Jacob shared his own thoughts also, about who Elizabeth was from his perspective.

Jacob invited everyone to the ranch house for a meal after the service to honor Elizabeth's wishes. Marianne and Nicole had prepared the meal, and Jacob, Carl and

Sam arranged seating and floral arrangements. The place reflected Elizabeth in every aspect.

It was a long day, and everyone was tired, especially James's sister and brother; Jacob invited them to stay for a few days. "You know, Elizabeth and James would like that, said Jacob and, we would like to have you, also."

The next morning, everyone carried on as usual, breakfast with the ranch hands in the dining hall, buffet style.

Chapter Forty-Four

Carl, Nicole and Sam returned to Ontario after a week. They knew Marianne and Jacob were more than capable of managing the ranch. Someday, they would move to the ranch; Perhaps after Sam finished high school. In the meantime, everything and everybody would continue as usual.

Nicole and Carl were sure about Marianne being capable of running the ranch with Jacob, except for Marianne, herself. It was a huge responsibility that frightened her. And then, there was Chris, her fiancée. There were a few letters from him waiting to be opened. He did not know about Elizabeth passing away; He did not know Marianne was now part of the role of caretaker of the ranch. Marianne opened one letter, read the contents, and continued to read two more. The first letter Chris was begging for Marianne to move to New Denmark, and in the last letter, he was expressing anger. If she didn't contact him within a week, he was breaking their engagement, and moving on without her.

Marianne was devastated about the whole situation. She felt everyone was controlling her life's direction, and she sobbed one whole night, after she sent Chris a responding letter.

The next morning, Jacob noticed Marianne's swollen, red eyes. Because she had told him about Chris, he didn't make any comments, and he helped her prepare breakfast.

As a matter of fact, Jacob made no comments at all, when he saw the pain and sadness in Marianne's eyes; They had a ranch to run.

"Marianne, said Jacob, one Friday night, will you go riding with me tomorrow night? I want to visit Elizabeth's grave, and I don't want to go alone."

"Yeah sure, said Marianne smiling, a good idea!"

It was good for Marianne and Jacob to go riding together. Marianne learned that she could trust Jacob, and she needed to unload her thoughts and feelings on someone. They rode to Elizabeth's and James' grave, got off their horse and stood in silence, briefly. Then, just as Jacob began to speak, Marianne was about to do the same. Jacob held back and let Marianne go first.

"You know, Jacob, it was a shock for me, when Auntie took the first stroke; I didn't see that her days were numbered; Did you?"

"Yes, sort of, but I hoped I was wrong." he replied. He paused, then he smoothed the ground with his boot, "You know Marianne, I suspected that Elizabeth knew, that's why she made her wishes known to us."

"You're right, Jacob, I guess; I just didn't want to see it." said Marianne.

They got back on their horses, and kept their thoughts to themselves, as they rode back to the house.

Once they got back, they both walked their horses to the stables. It was just getting dusk, and both Marianne and Jacob were hesitating to call it a night.

"Jacob, will you join me at the house; I really don't want to be alone?" said Marianne.

"I was hoping you'd offer an invitation; I don't feel like being alone either." added Jacob.

They made some popcorn, poured a glass of red wine and then, they sat on the loveseat relaxing, before the fireplace. Perhaps they were mesmerized by the dancing flames in the fireplace, or maybe, it was the wine that moved them to embracing and kissing each other. Their needs for each other were so great emotionally and physically, they gave in to them. They didn't even think about taking necessary precautions beforehand.

The next morning, they woke up in the living room. The fire had died in the fireplace, and the fire they experienced before they fell asleep, had died also.

"Good morning, Marianne." said Jacob peering into Marianne's face.

Marianne bolted upright. She realized that she wasn't wearing anything, and either was Jacob. They had pulled a throw over themselves, after they made out and fell asleep. Marianne grabbed her clothes and scurried to the bathroom. In the meantime, Jacob made some coffee. The fragrance wafted into the room, and together, they made breakfast. They sat together quietly for quite sometime before Jacob asked, "What's your agenda for today?"

Chapter Forty-Five

Christmas was just around the corner. Nicole and Marguerite were baking up a storm. Last year, Marianne got to help, and it was a big highlight of the season for the women. For the guys, it meant decorating the yards and the outsides of the respective houses as usual. Usually, all the family gathered to decorate the inside of the house, and of course the Christmas tree.

Sam woke up early one morning and looked outside. It wasn't daylight yet, and snow had fallen during the night, painting a picture like a Norman Rockwell winter scene. He got dressed and went outside with his camera. He wanted to share all that winter beauty with his sister.

When Nicole and Carl heard Sam in the kitchen, they decided to get up. "Sam, said Carl, why are you up so early?"

"Yeah," chimed in Nicole rubbing her eyes.

"When I woke up, said Sam, I looked outside; There was so much snow. Marianne loves the first snow, so I went outside with my camera, and I took some pictures, just for her."

"Oh honey, that is so sweet." said Nicole. Carl turned around because he had tears in his eyes; He missed Marianne so much.

That evening they called Marianne. Sam used his phone in his bedroom, Carl used the phone in the kitchen, and Nicole went to her bedroom phone. When Marianne heard the phone ring, she ran to it; She too, was so lonesome.

"Hello….., Jacob was calling from the front door, is anybody home?"

"Yeah, I am." answered Marianne starring at Jacob standing at the doorway. She was still feeling emotional after her phone call, and her eyes were still moist from her tears.

"Want some company?" he asked.

"Yeah sure, come in." Marianne needed some company. She made room for Jacob on the loveseat.

"I just got done talking to mom, dad and Sam; I felt so lonesome, and I fell apart; What brings you here?" she asked.

New Beginnings

"I was feeling out off sorts, so I thought I'd come over; Marianne, I want you to meet my mom and dad, and my sister, Irene; Could we do that, sometime?"

Marianne jumped up, she was excited, "Yeah, let's invite them over for supper!"

"I'll help you, let's see......." he said when Marianne reached close to him, and she kissed him. Jacob returned a passionate kiss.

Chapter Forty-Six

It was a Saturday night, and Jacob's family were having supper with him and Marianne at the ranch. They arrived a bit before supper, and together, they sat with Marianne and Jacob in the living room.

"Jacob told us about you coming here from Toronto to help your aunt; I can see she was a lucky lady." said Angela, Jacobs' mom.

"Well, I can say that I am the lucky one, added Marianne; I feel so blessed since I came here."

Jacob and his dad were having a conversation about the ranch, and Marianne noticed Irene, Jacobs' sister; She was so quiet. "Irene, let me show you and your mom around; There's so much to take in here." said Marianne.

After the informal introductions, they gathered in the dining room for supper. Jacob asked his dad to give thanks for the meal before they started. After the meal, Jacob said, "Mom, dad and Irene, come with me, Marianne will clean up for now."

"Irene and I are going to help Marianne." remarked Angela.

Jacob wanted to be the perfect host, but he knew his mom was not listening; He gave Marianne a look of exasperation and continued with his dad. There was a ball game on television, so Jacob and his dad enjoyed watching the game together. The women remained in the kitchen after cleaning up, and together, they got caught up in some girl talk.

"Jacob where are you going?" asked Marianne, when he walked over to the doorway, picking up his cowboy hat after their company left.

"Home, you look tired." He replied.

"I am, but don't go, not yet!" she said.

He returned his hat to the peg and, walked over to Marianne. He bent over to kiss her so lightly on her lips and, wrapped his arms around her.

Marianne responded with much need for affection, and together they spent the night in the living room. Again, they didn't take any necessary precautions before they engaged in lovemaking.

Chapter Forty-Seven

Marianne and Jacob decorated the ranch house, all the outbuildings and the yard for Christmas. While they were decorating the inside Christmas tree, Marianne remarked, "Jacob, it's so strange having Christmas, without snow!"

"Maybe for you, Marianne; It's all that I know about Christmas!" added Jacob smiling up at Marianne while she was putting an angel on the treetop.

"Ahh." cried Marianne as she fell from the step ladder. Jacob caught her and together they shared a little laugh, and a quick kiss, before he put her down onto the floor.

"We always get together with Grampie Sam and Marguerite for Christmas, it's gonna be different, now." said Marianne.

"Why don't we spend Christmas with my family?" suggested Jacob.

"Oh Jacob, that's a great idea!" exclaimed Marianne, and she planted a small kiss on his cheek.

"We always have a Christmas dinner with the ranch hands, and their family. Then, we have a party, playing Yankee Swap." added Jacob.

"On Christmas eve we go to Mass, and then we go home and exchange our gifts." said Marianne.

"We, Baptist people, don't have mass; We go to church Christmas eve; Then we go home. Mom and dad finish wrapping the gifts and then, they put them underneath the tree. That way, it looks like Santa came during the night."

Marianne pushed Jacob to the love seat, and together they hit each other with a cushion, all the while laughing.

"Look at that tree." said Jacob.

"Why?" said Marianne.

"It's beaming, with love!" he replied

"Yeah." replied Marianne.

They made love, freshened up with a shower; Then, they went for a short ride on the horses.

Marianne looked at her alarm clock, it was three forty-five am. She felt sick and dizzy. She hurried off to the bathroom, realizing that she was experiencing morning sickness. After getting sick, she looked into the mirror, and said "You're pregnant, Marianne." Then, she tried to vomit again, from an empty stomach. "Eat some soda crackers." she thought. Her friend told her it worked, at least for her. Marianne went to the pantry, found some soda crackers and she started eating them, when she heard Jacob. Breakfast for the ranch hands was at five am. and now it was four thirty. She washed her face with cold water, got dressed and joined Jacob in the kitchen.

"You're late; I got the coffee started." he said.

"Give me a few minutes, and breakfast will be ready." she assured him, trying to hide her morning sickness.

While the guys and Jacob were exchanging the latest happenings on the ranch, and their plans for the day, they did not notice that Marianne had stormed off to the bathroom. After the men left Jacob went looking for Marianne. He found her in the bathroom hugging the flush.

"Pregnant, are your sure?" questioned Jacob.

"Yeah, I'm almost sure." stated Marianne; Then, she started to vomit again, and Jacob left for the kitchen.

When Marianne came into the kitchen, Jacob was running a hand through his hair; He was lost for words and, stood looking at Marianne.

"Say something!" she exclaimed.

"We're having a baby!" he said with a grin as he approached her. She was feeling sick again and, resorted to the bathroom.

"I didn't mean to laugh at you." said Jacob.

"Yeah, you did!" retorted Marianne.

Jacob suggested that Marianne should take some deep breaths and relax with him at the kitchen table. They had a lot to talk about. "We should be having a baby in September." said Jacob.

"Yeah." responded Marianne with an odd look on her face.

"You know, we did not take precautions, and it was inevitable. I am happy, aren't you?" questioned Jacob.

Marianne looked at Jacob, and she said, "After this morning sickness." and she stormed off to the bathroom.

Marianne wanted to digest the fact that she and Jacob were going to have a baby before they made any announcements to their family. First, they went to the hospital to have a doctor confirm the pregnancy. Then, they went to the local restaurant to kinda' celebrate positive results. Jacob and Marianne made an announcement the next morning at breakfast to the ranch hands. All the guys cheered and whistled.

Chapter Forty-Eight

The phone was ringing off the wall on a Saturday morning, and Jacob hurried to answer it.

"Hello Jacob, said Angela, I expected Marianne to answer."

"She is in the shower right now, he replied. Do you want her to call you back?"

"No, no said Angela, your dad and I thought, it would be nice to have you and Marianne in for supper."

"That would be great, I'll ask Marianne, and we'll call you back." replied Jacob.

"Ok. said Angela, and they both hung up.

"Did I hear the phone ring?" asked Marianne as she came into the kitchen wearing a bath sheet only.

"It was my mom, she invited us over for supper!"

"Great, will you tell everyone about the baby, Jacob; I'd rather not?" asked Marianne.

"No, Jacob replied, we will tell them, ok! Marianne nodded with her approval, and she smiled.

"Marianne, said Jacob starring into her eyes and holding her at a distance, I'm moving in with you!"

Marianne starred back at Jacob, "A good idea." she replied with a big grin on her face; Then, she left the room to get dressed.

"Pregnant, you're pregnant!" exclaimed Nicole, after Marianne told her mother the news over the phone.

"Mom, if I knew you would've reacted like you just did, I wouldn't have told you." said Marianne.

"What about college?" questioned Nicole.

"I don't want to go to college, mom." stated Marianne.

Carl heard Nicole on the phone; He figured it had to be Marianne.

"Nicole, is that Marianne, let me talk to her?" he asked.

"So, what's up, Marianne?" asked Carl.

Jacob and I are having a baby." said Marianne.

"Are you happy?" asked Carl.

"Yeah dad, we are." replied Marianne.

"If you and Jacob are happy, so am I." Carl said.

"Where is Sam?" asked Marianne.

"You would know, he is with Sarah, of course." said Carl.

"Would you tell Sam, he's gonna be an uncle, and would you tell Grampie and Marguerite, please dad; Got to go, Love you!"

Jacob was sitting by Marianne's side, and from the sound of her conversation, he decided to remain quiet.

"You're quiet." said Marianne to Jacob.

"Listening to your conversation, I thought it was best." he responded, then he planted a kiss on Marianne's forehead.

"My mom is so controlling, I hate it." she said, still fuming.

"But she loves you, right." he added.

"Yeah, lets' talk about something else"; Marianne didn't want to talk about her mother.

Chapter Forty-Nine

The New year brought new beginnings; Sammy was graduating from High School in June, and Marianne was having a baby in August. On July the first, Nicole and Carl were moving to Southern California permanently.

Carl and Nicole took a long weekend at Easter to visit Stella and their family in New Denmark. They always kept in touch by phone, however they needed a few days to catch up on all the latest news. Stella wouldn't complain about her health on the phone and, Carl and Nicole were aware of that.

The day they arrived was sunny, but a bit chilly, still. Stella was outside in the yard, waiting for them when they drove up. She was all smiles, and she had a Border Collie on a leash, bouncing about.

"Hi Mom, whose dog?" Carl asked

"Mine, Aaron gave him to me. He couldn't keep him." said Stella as she walked to the door.

"Come in, come in, I'll put the kettle on, and we can have a lunch." said Stella as she walked in with Fido the dog.

When Stella unfastened the dog's leash, the dog went directly to the front of the wood stove; Stella had a cozy fire on.

"Have a seat, said Stella as she started to get some wood to stoke the fire.

"Mom, you have a seat, and I'll do that! exclaimed Carl. Then, after adding some wood to the fire, he took the coffee pot and made some coffee; He opened the fridge and found some coffee cream and some cheese; Oh mom, you made some coffee cake; Let's have some of that."

"Sure Carl, get some small plates; They're in the same place." said Stella.

Once Carl got seated, they started to catch up on the latest news.

"Mom, when did you get Fido, you never told us about her?" asked Carl. Nicole sat quietly sipping on her hot coffee waiting to hear the story about Fido.

"Well, Aaron moved into an apartment, and he wasn't allowed to have pets; I was more than happy to have her." replied Stella.

"Fido is a girl, why does she have that name?" pursued Carl.

"Well, when Aaron was at the pet store, he fell in love with her. A little girl was calling her Fido, and so she became Fido!" explained Stella. Now tell me some news; I'm sure there's lot's happening. How are Marianne and Sammy doing?" Stella still called Sam, Sammy.

"Well Sam is still in school doing great; He is still going with Sarah." said Carl looking at Nicole as she continued to sit quietly.

"What about Marianne?" asked Stella.

Nicole starred at Carl and, made motion for him to answer Stella. "She is still in California; She and Jacob are having a baby."

Stella gasped and put her wrinkled hand to her mouth. "A baby, little Marianne is having a baby! she said with tears spilling from her eyes. When is she due?"

Nicole replied, "August." and she put her head down. She still wasn't happy about it all; She started to get up to clear the table.

"Nicole, said Stella, sit, I want to hear more; Carl, get us some more coffee."

It was a long weekend, for sure, especially for Nicole; She was anxious to get home. Carl, on the other hand, needed to check Stella's place from every angle, the house, shed and yard. He would make the necessary repairs, so he made mental notes regarding the house and his mom living there still, alone.

Stella invited Peter, Neils and their families in for supper, and for socializing, as usual; These times were the highlights of their visit; Even Aaron would be home for the long weekend.

Chapter Fifty

Carl submitted his notice to quit City Construction. He wanted to give enough notice to be available for Sam's Graduation. Then, he and Nicole were planning their move to California, after the first of July.

Nicole made plans for her Realty Company with her staff. She promoted Ellen, her reliable assistant to the Charge position, of her Company. Every other staff member needed to be moved up to another level, and she needed to hire someone new, besides.

They made plans to rent their house; They were undecided about their future so, by renting, they would be ready for the unexpected down the road.

Sam and Marguerite were saddened to see their family move; However, Sam always believed in "What will be, will be."

Sam Jr. moved in with his grandparents; He was attending a Community College in the fall, and of course, he wanted to stay near Sarah.

On July first, Sam and his girlfriend Sarah, Sam Senior and Marguerite were saying their good-byes to Carl and Nicole at the Toronto International Airport. And hours later, Carl and Nicole would be saying, "Hello" to Marianne and Jacob.

Marianne and Jacob had cleaned and polished the red convertible before they left to pick up her parents. They mowed the grass, pruned the shrubs, and made sure everything was lovely and inviting. They wanted to make a good impression, regarding the care of the ranch house, and the surroundings. Elizabeth was like that, always impressing and inviting, so they needed to keep up her ideals.

Marianne was all smiles when she saw her mom and dad entering the gates of the airport; Jacob stood alongside of her, smiling as well.

Nicole reached out to touch Marianne's protruding belly, just when the baby was moving at the same time.

"Did you feel that mom?" asked Marianne.

"Sure did!" exclaimed Nicole.

"Come on, let's go home!" said Jacob; "Supper, and a few surprises are waiting for you at the ranch!"

Upon arriving at the ranch, Nicole exclaimed, "Love it!" Jacob and Marianne had some renovations made to the ranch. The front entrance was moved to allow for the addition of a formal dining room and Foyer. The entrance for the ranch hands was moved to the side of the building.

Nicole, being in real estate, marvelled at the changes, and just stood there.

"Mom, you gotta see what we did inside." said Marianne, as she motioned for everyone to follow.

"What do you think, Mom, Dad?"

"We love it!" said Nicole and Carl simultaneously.

"Now, for your bedroom, said Marianne, just follow us."

Nicole was in awe, and Carl only said "Thanks." and he then put his hands up and exclaimed; I don't know about you guys, I'm hungry!"

"Good, said Jacob, Marianne and I cooked up a feast this morning."

"And we're eating in the new dining room!" added Marianne.

Chapter Fifty-One

Nicole walked down the hallway, and found Marianne bent over; She was experiencing pain in her lower back. "You're in labor!"

Oh, God!" exclaimed Nicole as she touched Marianne on her arm.

"Mom, it hurts; I need Jacob!" responded Marianne.

"Jacob is busy, I'll get your dad to go get him; I'm driving you to the hospital, now!" instructed Nicole.

"But mom, Jacob will take me!" said Marianne, still bent over in pain.

Nicole wasn't listening to Marianne; "Come on, Marianne; Get in that car, Jacob will be at the hospital later!"

Marianne had no choice in the matter, and sure enough, Jacob arrived at the hospital later. He stayed by Marianne's side until they took Marianne into the delivery room. He paced the floors, until he heard a baby's cry, their baby's cry. A nurse came to his side, and said, "You can go in now." Marianne was sitting up, all smiles with her swaddling baby. He walked over to her, and planted a light kiss on her forehead, and reached to touch the baby; Marianne passed the baby over to him and said, "Jacob, we have a boy!"

Then, the attending nurse walked toward Jacob and said, "Gotta take your baby to the nursery now, and Marianne you need to rest." Jacob gave Marianne a quick hug and a small kiss; He was going home, a very happy man.

He met Nicole at the front door, waiting to give him a hug; "Congratulations, dad!" she said. Carl was soon by their side with Congratulations and an exchange of "High-Five" with Jacob.

"Time for a coffee, said Nicole; We want to hear everything about that new baby, and Marianne." She placed three mugs of very hot coffee, sandwiches, and home-made donuts on the table. She figured Jacob must be hungry, and she wanted to occupy all the time necessary to hear about Marianne and the baby.

Later, Jacob went out to buy a huge arrangement of flowers for Marianne and then, he went to visit her.

When he walked into her room, she was walking towards him, because she heard his footsteps as he neared her door. She was all smiles, as she took the arrangement from him, and set it on her night table. She anticipated his hug and kiss.

"Come with me," said Marianne, as she took his hand, and led him to the nurses' station; "Would you bring our baby to my room?" she asked a nurse. Then, both Jacob and Marianne followed the nurse back to her room. Marianne took a seat in a rocking chair; Then, the nurse placed the baby in her arms and, left the room. Jacob got down on one knee, gave Marianne a little kiss, and likewise to their baby.

"I'm coming in tomorrow, said Jacob; We gotta get this baby registered with a name."

"Sure, will we still call him Alexander?" asked Marianne. They had already decided on the name for a boy.

"Alexander, it is!" expressed Jacob smiling. He picked up their baby's little hand, held on to it, smiled at Marianne, and kissed her ever so gently.

"By the way, Marianne, did you call your brother, and your grandparents?' asked Jacob as he stood to his feet.

"Yes, Grampie was so excited, I heard him call Marguerite, and Sam. He yelled so loud, I had to take the phone away, from my ear." replied Marianne.

"What about Grammy Stella?" questioned Jacob.

"Yes, I did, I can just see her face, now!" exclaimed Marianne.

"I called my mom and dad, added Jacob. Mom answered the phone, and she said she would pass the news about the baby to dad and Sissy; By the way, I hired Sissy to take your place in the kitchen." said Jacob.

"A good idea, Jacob, commented Marianne, I love you."

Chapter Fifty-Two

It wasn't long before Marianne and Nicole were butting heads. Nicole's intentions were legitimate, but to Marianne, she was stepping past her boundaries. Whenever baby Alex cried, Nicole rushed in to get him, especially if she was nearby. "Mom, it's not your place to pick the baby up whenever; I'm his mother, ok."

"Sorry, I was only helping, you know that!" exclaimed Nicole.

"Well, the next time he cries, said Marianne, I'll be the one to get him!"

Then, it happened one day when Marianne was in the shower. Alex cried, and cried, until his tears covered his face, and he was so sweaty. Nicole, despite what Marianne said, went to his room to see why he was crying. He had vomited on his bedsheet, and his face and hair was covered. Nicole cleaned him up and took him to the rocking chair to comfort him. When Marianne walked by the nursery, she saw her mom with baby Alex; She was livid with anger. She yelled at her mom, and Nicole yelled back. Carl happened to be walking past, and he walked into the room. He took Alex from Nicole and stood back; "You're frightening him, all that yelling!" he said and, walked out of the room leaving Nicole and Marianne, perplexed.

When Marianne joined Jacob in their room that night, they both knew they had to resolve the issues between her and her mother. "Marianne, said Jacob, we're moving into the bunk house, tomorrow."

"Why?" asked Marianne; She started to cry.

"After todays' incident, I know, we gotta do something!" he said putting a hand on Marianne's shoulder.

"Are you mad at me?" asked Marianne; She started to cry even more.

"No," he said, and he hugged her lovingly.

"I've been thinking that we should build our own house, said Jacob; What do you think?"

"Our own house, Jacob, but where?" replied Marianne.

"Somewhere up the road, near the sheep farm." he replied.

"I have always loved that spot; I can picture it now." she added.

"I talked to your dad, said Jacob and, with his help, we should have the house finished by Christmas!"

"Oh Jake, I love you!" said Marianne reaching up to kiss him. He returned the kiss.

Chapter Fifty-Three

"Wow, I love it; Can't wait to move in!" exclaimed Marianne, when she came by the new house one day.

"So, your old dad still has what it takes to build a house!" said Carl, as he looked from Marianne to the house.

"Oh dad, you're not old, older, but not old." she said. Then, she walked over to him, put an arm around him and said, "Love you, Dad!"

Back at the house, Nicole was baking up a storm for the holidays. Marianne joined her mother later, until Alex woke up from his nap. She changed him, fed him and then, she put him in his highchair in the kitchen. Then, she continued to help her mom.

They baked everything from doughnuts, cookies, breads and of course, Tortierre.

The place smelled so good by the time the ranch hands, including Jake, came in for supper. It was just like old times when Elizabeth was chief cook; Elizabeth would never be forgotten.

On the weekend, the men decorated the outside of their home, and the women decorated inside. Then, when the decorating was finished, they gathered together for family time in the living room in front of the fireplace; They shared stories, test tasted some of the baked goodies with mugs of hot chocolate. Even baby Alex contributed with the entertainment and fun.

Samuel flew into California a week before Christmas to enjoy the holidays, and to help Marianne and Jacob move into their new house. He was thrilled seeing his nephew, and how he had grown.

Alexander enjoyed all the attention he got from his uncle, and of course, he performed a few antics that made Samuel laugh.

"You know Sis, I missed you so much!" said Sam as he approached her from behind, startling her. Marianne jumped and they both laughed, giving each other a hug.

"How's everything going in Toronto; How's Gramps and Marguerite?" Marianne was talking so fast; Sam didn't have much chance to answer all her questions.

The transition from the main house to the new one went well; Marianne and Nicole had prepared a huge meal of homemade bread, Tortierre and apple pie for everyone. It was a great time, especially since Sam was with them.

On Christmas Eve, everyone went to Mass; Then, they gathered at Marianne's and Jacob's place. Nicole encouraged everyone to help her in the dining room with a late-night meal.

Marianne and Jacob took Alexander to his bedroom and tucked him in his crib. While they stood admiring their baby, they exchanged a quick kiss; Then, they joined everyone in the dining room. After the meal, Marianne announced, "Ok, time to open our gifts!"

It was a special evening of making memories, taking pictures, and having fun with all the family.

Everyone stayed over with Jacob and Marianne; In the morning after brunch, phone calls were made to Grammie Stella, and to Grampie Sam and Marguerite. A lot of tears were shed, some happy, and some sad. Again, baby Alex was the highlight of their conversations.

Chapter Fifty-Four

When Sam was leaving California after Christmas, there were many exchanges of hugs, well wishes, and a few tears. His dad drove him to the airport, and they had an opportunity to talk man to man. They both needed this time together in a big way.

Sam senior and Marguerite picked him up at The Toronto International Airport; Sarah was at home waiting and watching the clock. She was missing Sam to no end.

In June, Sam was graduating from Community College with a degree in Carpentry, and Sara was graduating from High School. While Sam apprenticed with a reputable Company, Sarah made plans to attend Bible School in California, despite the fact, her parents wanted her to attend a prestigious college in Toronto.

"I've got my mind made up, she said. "Sam and I will be getting married, and we will be living in California."

Sarah's parents were not too happy, but they knew they couldn't change her mind. And Sarah knew that her parents would be continually interfering in her relationship with Sam.

After Sam finished his apprentice in Toronto, he and Sarah drove to New Denmark; Sam wanted his grandmother to meet his future wife. He missed spending time with his grandmother.

The drive was pleasurable for both Sam and Sarah; It was their first time away from their families, alone.

"I'm gad, we are taking this time together with your grandmother; I can't wait to experience life in the country!" said Sarah.

"You will love it, it is quiet; And grandmothers' house is so unique. She still uses a wood stove, and she has a dog, too." added Sam.

When they drove up Stella's drive, her dog came to greet them, with his tail wagging, oh so fast. Stella heard the dog bark, and she told him to stop; The dog looked at Stella, refrained from barking, and bounced around Sam and Sarah happily.

"Come in, come in," said Stella. She was waiting for a hug from Sam, and for introductions with regards to Sarah.

Sam was very much like his dad, Carl. While he tended to his grandmother's yard, and made repairs to her house and shed, Sarah baked with Stella, learned how to crochet, and knit. She was thoroughly enjoying herself. Sometimes Sam took them to Grand Falls to shop at the local grocery store and all the shops. They ate meals at the local restaurants and, they enjoyed all the social aspects of the community.

While spending time with Stella, Sam and Sarah planned their future wedding. They both decided to have a countryside wedding in Stella's front yard some day.

Stella was ecstatic with their plans. She hugged both Sarah and Sam, perhaps a little tight, and she shed a few happy tears with them.

"Now Gram, our wedding day is going to happen, right here with you, and all our family; Right in front of those birch trees!" said Sam.

"Ok", said Stella, and she walked over to hug them again; Sarah first, and then she hugged Sam.

Time flew by quickly and Sam and Sarah were returning to California very soon. Sam decided to take a scenic route to Houlton Maine. He wanted to impress Sarah, and he was leaving his car in storage at the airport.

Chapter Fifty-Five

Carl and Nicole sat in Elizabeth's red convertible waiting for Sam and Sarah. It was a warm and sunny day; A day to drive with the top down on the convertible. When they arrived at the ranch, Jacob, and Marianne was waiting for them just outside the door. Upon getting out of the car, Sarah was in awe, and her mouth flew open as she scanned the sights as far as she could.

"Come on Sarah, you remember Marianne and Jacob?" questioned Sam, and before Sarah could answer him, he was asking about baby Alex.

Nicole and Carl grabbed some luggage and urged everyone to go inside. Sarah was still in awe and, was lost for words. She politely followed Sam into the living room.

Marianne was about to serve refreshments, just as Alex announced to everyone that he was awake. Marianne was quick to go to him, but Jacob stopped her, "Marianne,

I'll get him, and he left the room before Marianne could object.

Jacob lifted Alex out of his crib, put him on the changing table, and changed him into one of his cutest outfits. All the while, Alex was proclaiming, "Da, Da, Da."

Everyone focused their eyes on Alex when Jacob came out with him in his arms. Sam walked over to them, put his hands out toward Alex, and Alex quickly turned away. It had been a few months since Sam left California, and Alex had forgotten who he was.

"You just wait, said Marianne, soon Alex will want your full attention, Sam; He is always shy at first." And Marianne was right, within a short time Alex stuck by his Uncle Sam like glue.

The men went outside to sit on the porch and, Nicole showed Sarah around the house. "First, I'll show you your room, said Nicole. And, we have a few bathrooms, so whenever you feel like freshening up, you make yourself at home."

"Just then, Sarah heard some loud voices. "I hear some loud voices." she said.

"Oh, said Nicole, we have ranch hands coming in around six; They have supper in the dining hall after they leave the fields. Marianne and I prepare their meals and, clean up later; Why don't you take this time for yourself?"

"Okay." said Sarah, and she was off.

The next day, Sam got up early to help his dad. For the time being, Sam was helping his dad, maintaining the ranch, and assisting the ranch hands. Then, after he acquired the skills of being a charge person, his dad could take on his new position of management.

Sarah, on the other hand would assist Nicole and Marianne with meals and housekeeping. She had lots to learn.

After supper, Sarah helped Sam move into Jakes' old bunkhouse. Sarah was remaining at the house until she was off to University in September.

Like Marianne, Sarah had to learn the responsibilities of a cook, and housekeeper. By the end of the day, she was exhausted, so she relaxed with Sam at the bunkhouse in the evenings. Sometimes they joined Carl and Nicole at the main house. And sometimes, they visited with Marianne and Jake. Baby Alex was a real delight, performing his antics.

Sometimes, they went horseback riding after Sarah learned how. Sarah was constantly in awe; There was so much activity to experience on the ranch. Every day was always a new day.

Chapter Fifty-Six

When Sarah left for university, it was with reservations on both Sam's part and her part. Because it was a four-hour drive from the ranch, Sarah stayed on Campus during the week.

Sarah enjoyed the theory regarding the courses; She always liked the challenges they offered. She liked the rapport of fellow-students; Therefore, it did not take long before she felt a sense of belonging, and right at home on campus.

Her only problem was the guilt she felt whenever Sam called; Even though Sam called every night, she worried about their relationship.

Sam felt a twinge of jealousy often; He tried to hide it, but Sarah was quick to take notice. So, when Sarah came home on the weekend, she continually reassured him, there was no room for jealousy in their relationship.

On Saturday mornings, both Sarah and Sam worked as usual on the ranch, however, after supper it was totally their time. They spent those times together at Sam's Bunkhouse. On Sunday morning, they attended church faithfully, visiting with family until Sarah had to return to Campus. For both Sarah and Sam, this time was very difficult. Sarah usually had to keep her tears in check, and Sam had to be careful about his moods.

Christmas was arriving, and Sam and Sarah could hardly wait for the holidays; They were going to Toronto to visit with her parents, and with Sam's Grandparents. Then, they were travelling to New Denmark to visit with Stella. It would be Sarah's first Christmas in the country. Sam wanted Sarah to experience finding a real Christmas tree, making snow angels, and helping Stella with all the Christmas preparations. They would be making lasting memories.

Soon after Christmas, they were back in California, getting back to their usual routines. Sarah got her engagement ring for Christmas with a proposed date for their wedding, July the first. They planned on a Fall wedding, but because they wanted to allow themselves time for a honeymoon, they changed their dates.

Chapter Fifty-Seven

Sarah was so excited about her upcoming wedding. She shopped for a wedding dress with Nicole, and sometimes with Marianne. From one of the boutiques, she settled on an off-white satin gown, with a cowl neckline. It was sleeveless and it had an empire waist band accented with embroidery and pearls. The skirt was long and straight with side slits edged with embroidery and pearls to match the waist band. She wasn't wearing a veil, but she was having her hair styled in a smooth chignon entwined with beads and white satin ribbons. She settled on slingback shoes in off-white satin. Then, all she had left to buy was her jewellery, a bouquet, and off course, a leg band.

Sarah could hardly contain her excitement, let alone concentrate on her studies.

At the end of June, Sam and Sarah flew to Houlton Maine, to pick up their car. Then, they travelled to New Denmark to visit Stella and then, made plans to decorate

Stella's yard, and arrange seating for the wedding family and close friends. They were not having a regular reception; They wanted their wedding ceremony to reflect a relaxed, enjoyable atmosphere. They were, however, serving light refreshments.

Carl and Nicole, Marianne, and Jake, with Alexander, flew from the airport in California to The Houlton Airport, a few days before the wedding. They wanted to assure Stella that, she didn't need to worry about any pre-wedding preparations. And they wanted Stella to enjoy her great grandson, Alex; She hadn't seen him yet, and he was almost a year old. Sam's cousin, Aaron was the best man and Marianne was the maid of honor.

The words from the minister, "I now pronounce you husband and wife," created feelings of pure joy for Sarah and Sam, and when the minister continued, "You may kiss the bride," both Sarah and Sam embraced in each others' arm and kissed so tenderly with all their love.

After a lot of hugs, and well wishes, the happy couple left for their honeymoon.

They drove to the popular hotel, Pres Du Lac, and booked into the honeymoon suite for the night. Then the next morning, after breakfast, they travelled to Saint John, New Brunswick to board the Digby Ferry to Halifax. They wanted to tour the seaside, and boardwalks to Pier Twenty-One. That was where Carl was detained with his brother, after arriving from Denmark with his mom and siblings.

Once they arrived in Halifax, they booked into the Fenwick Hotel and relaxed with each other, and they made love again and again. After a couple of days, they boarded the ferry to Prince Edward Island. Near a beach, they booked into a rustic cottage for three days; It was like heaven, viewing the sunrises and sunsets. They shopped markets, museums, and boutiques; They ate from the finest restaurants and outside cafés, except when they prepared their own meals, together, at the cottage.

After three days in Prince Edward Island, they boarded the ferry to the mainland. They were anxious to get back to California, so they drove to Houlton, Maine, and put their car in storage again. They boarded a plane, and soon they arrived in California.

Once they arrived in California, they booked into a hotel and relaxed for a few days by themselves; They needed time to discuss their new beginnings.

"Sam, said Sarah, I'm not going back to Bible College."

"Sarah, why not?" questioned Sam, as he put his hands around her waist, looking deeply into her eyes.

"I don't want to spend my nights, without you and……….." Sarah didn't get to finish saying what she wanted to; She wanted to tell Sam that she was pregnant.

"But Sarah, what will your parents say?" asked Sam running his hands through his hair.

"I don't care what they think; For once, I'm following my own dream, and that is to be by your side; I love you, Sam!"

"I love you too, Sarah." Sam replied and kissed her passionately. Sarah decided to tell Sam later about being pregnant.

Chapter Fifty-Eight

Like Marianne, Sarah found it very difficult working with Nicole, and she complained to Sam every night after supper.

"Well, what do you want me to do?" questioned Sam; Sam was tired, and he didn't want to take sides between his mom and his wife. He had forgotten how his sister could not get along with his bossy, overbearing mom.

Early, one morning, Sarah woke up sick; She was leaning over the flush when Sam walked in; "Sarah, you're sick", he said, and then Sarah turned towards him, and she said, "I am pregnant!"

Sam was speechless only briefly, and he gave a little jump, and sounded a "Yeah!"; He couldn't wait to share the news.

"Sarah, you don't have to work today, get some rest; I'll get some breakfast, and head over to the ranch." Sam gave her a quick kiss and was off.

After work, Sam sauntered over to the bunk house, with a lightness in his spirit; His dad had offered him a proposal that would resolve issues for both Grammie Stella, and themselves.

Sarah met Sam in the doorway; She had prepared his favorite meal, fried Steak with mushroom and onions, gravy, mashed potatoes and corn on the cob.

"So, how was your day, Sarah?" questioned Sam.

"Great, responded Sarah, after I ate a few soda crackers."

"Sarah, Dad told me that Grammie Stella has been very tired lately, and out of sorts." Sarah was listening intently, as Sam continued, "Would you be happy making our future in New Denmark?"

Sarah walked over close to Sam, gave him a gentle kiss, and replied, "I would!".

Sam picked Sarah up off her feet, and he carried her to their bedroom. They made passionate love, until Sam blurted out, "We fly away this weekend!"

Then, Sarah nodded with an approval, and they continued their lovemaking.

On the weekend Sarah and Sam flew to Houlton Airport, picked up their car, and drove to New Denmark for their new beginnings. Eight months later, baby Becky was born, and Sam and Sarah lived happily ever after!

www.ingramcontent.com/pod-product-compliance
Lightning Source LLC
LaVergne TN
LVHW021714060526
838200LV00050B/2666